LOVE DOCTOR

LOGAN CHANCE

For Paula

I do things like get in a taxi and say, "The library, and step on it."

David Foster Wallace

A book must be the axe for the frozen sea within us.

Franz Kafka

Rose

"You don't start out writing good stuff. You start out writing crap and thinking it's good stuff, and then gradually you get better at it. That's why I say one of the most valuable traits is persistence."
— *Octavia E. Butler*

MAYBE I SHOULDN'T BE a writer. Well, technically, I'm not—yet—but becoming an author is in my ten year plan. Get a Husky, name her Thumbelina, and become an author by the time I'm thirty, those are my lofty goals. I'm running short on time. However, since joining this erotic writers group, I'm not so sure about aspiring to publish a novel. Maybe it should remain a secret hobby, because I'll tell you, writing is hard. Writing sex is even harder. Having it picked apart and dissected is excruciating. I'd rather shove the tiny black stirrers peeking out of everyone's coffee cups under my fingernails than continue to have the four people sitting with me in *Carl's Coffee* analyze my technique. Or lack thereof.

"I'm telling you, *member* is just not a sexy word for a man's penis," Pru Palmer, published author, scoffs with undisguised disgust in her brown eyes. "Is it in a club? No, it's a dick."

Uncomfortable with her criticism, and maybe a bit envious at the way she effortlessly says dick, I shift in my black leather chair while three sets of eyes study me like a specimen under a microscope at our early morning meetup for today. "Yes, well, I was trying to change things up," I defend myself. I mean, I didn't have a lot to work with in five hundred words.

"Change it to dick," she advises, arrogance lacing every word as she lifts her caramel latte for a sip. Her smoke shadowed eye winks at me. "Maybe then your sex scenes won't be so tame."

Ouch. Once a week, for three months, I've gathered with these people for creative writing exercises, and I'm still not used to the non-sugar coated critique from Pru and her overarched eyebrows. Obviously, I know member isn't sexy, neither is shaft, but I can't write dick a million times. She pumps out bestselling books faster than the hero in my book can pump his 'member' into the heroine, so maybe I should heed her advice and stop agonizing over word choice.

"You've got immense natural talent," Christian, our organizer, tells me, shrugging off Pru's judgement and pushing his glasses further up his nose. I don't miss Pru's minuscule eyebrow rise at his praise. "How is your manuscript progressing?"

"Good," I answer as vague as possible. "I'm almost done."

At some point, I'll have to share with them, but other than sex scene snippets, I'm not ready to divulge what my novel is about just yet.

Thankfully, he moves on to Rebecca, a wisp of a girl with pink streaks in her blonde hair and a tongue as sharp as a razor blade. "Don't even try to tell me rod isn't ok," she directs at Pru. "Your ghost writer needs to learn to use a thesaurus."

"Rebecca," Christian chastises, futilely trying to stop the storm brewing. He'd have more luck stopping the earth from turning. Rebecca lapses into the same tirade I've heard since I joined—there's no way Pru can publish as often as she does without outside help. I'm beginning to wonder if she isn't right. Pru's readers don't seem to question the plausibility of whether or not producing a novel every few weeks is actually possible, but I do.

"Well, it's true," Rebecca continues, not backing down. "She has everyone fooled, but people can't stay blind forever. Why are you even here?"

Her words ricochet off Pru, leaving no dents. "I like to give back."

Christian wrangles control of the conversation and the critique of Rebecca's story about bear shifters becomes the focus. In the midst of debating whether supplying condoms in a forest is indeed necessary, my phone vibrates. I glance down at a text from my boss, Dr. Declan Sincock. Yes, that's really his name. And how fitting it is for all six feet plus, hotter than magma inches of him.

I need you to bring me a blueberry muffin top, his message reads.

Just the top, Rose.

T.O.P.

I like the top. No bottom.

Dr. Sincock and I are still in the getting to know you phase, and somehow, in the two months I've worked for him, he has managed to burrow so far under my skin, he lives there. I can't shed him. Of all the days to request a beheaded muffin, he'd pick today. Normally, on Thursday's, Dr. Sincock always arrives late, or I wouldn't have agreed to Christian's schedule change.

Just so I understand correctly, I type back: You would like an unattached muffin top?

"Yes," is his swift reply. "Top is always best. It's my favorite."

Immediately, my imagination conjures up a new scene for my novel with my hero, Eclan, on top of Annette: vicious red welts, from where she marked him, stretch down his corded back while his hips thrust, driving into her. It's so clear in my mind's eye, I can even see the tightening of his rounded ass cheeks as his ferocity intensifies. I jot down 'angry sex' on a sticky note and slide it in the pocket of my slacks before waiting for a lull in bear shifter orgies to excuse myself.

"I'll get right on it," I send back.

If he wants a half muffin, then that's what he'll get. I may be a questionable writer, but I'm a damn good personal assistant. Even if his requests are bizarre.

Last week, I spent an hour searching for a 'hot buttered biscuit dripping with honey,' only to find it still sitting on his desk, uneaten, an hour later. Rather than ask him about it when he returned from a meeting, I wrote a steamy breakfast scene with Eclan, shirtless and barefoot, licking drips of bees nectar from Annette's nipples while I devoured his biscuit. He doesn't know that, though.

"Hurry, please," he replies.

I slide my purse on my shoulder and stand. "Sorry, I have to get going."

"No problem," Christian says. "See you next week."

On my way out, a quick search of the internet reveals a bakery about ten minutes away. After retrieving the muffin, I drive to the medical building where Dr. Sincock practices sex therapy.

"Good morning," Katrina, the gatekeeper at the information desk, greets me when I step into the quiet lobby. The sun pours in through the big, bay windows and I pass by a large potted plant in the middle of the tiled floor.

"Morning." I give her a little wave, hustling to the elevator.

I punish the circular silver button with a little extra jab as payback for the way Dr. Sincock so easily pushes mine. On my ascent to the fifth floor, I map out the last few chapters of my novel in my head. Honestly, I'm not sure how it will end. I'm not an outline writer, and right now, Annette and Eclan currently have an obstacle in their way—he's her boss. Maybe they don't live happily ever after, who knows.

My heels click against the marble floor as I hurry to the office, drop my bag at my desk, and then rap on his door with a pink Magnificent Muffin bag in my hand.

"Come in," his deep voice beckons.

When I enter, I brace myself for the Sincock effect. It's an effect he's had on me since I sat down in his office for the obligatory interview. I wasn't prepared for him to be so handsome my nipples became steel juts of lust or the first question to be whether I liked avocado.

When I said yes, he unexpectedly pushed a button I didn't know I had by cringing at my answer and saying we could continue anyway. It was twenty minutes of damp panties and irritation that turned into ten chapters when I got back to my house.

I've never had anyone trigger me the way Dr. Sincock does. I'm in a constant state of haterousal. I hate that I'm oddly attracted to someone who is off limits and loathes avocados. They're a superfood, how can he not be an advocate?

Mossy green eyes track me as I cross to the glossy desk he sits behind. "Breakfast is served," I quip. I place the bag down and pull extra napkins for him from my pocket.

"Thank you," he responds with a charming grin before placing his finger on the button. "Thought I might die from hunger before you got back."

My eyes flit to the protein bar sitting next to his coffee mug. It's like I can literally feel the button being depressed. My smile is as forced as the solar stickman gadget pedaling away beside his monitor. I want to swoosh all the neatly stacked piles of paper off his desk, climb across, wrap his silver tie around my fist and wipe that smirk off his face with my tongue.

I'm not sure why he gets to me so much. His requests aren't that far from the norm of what I encountered at my previous job. My last boss, God rest his soul, the CEO of Westerhouse Puppy Modeling Agency had me dog sit at his house on the regular. And I did it, without complaint. Usually, I'm very eager to please, because I like knowing what my boss needs before he can express it. Until now.

I'm sure Dr. Sincock would equate my trigger ready buttons he's been able to activate so easily with some sort of sexual repression. And maybe he'd be right, he's the sex expert. I'm sure he'd know exactly how to set my inner slut free. She's inside me, living a very chaste existence.

The sound of crumpling paper permeates throughout the office as he removes his life support from the bag. Just so you know, he looks nowhere near close to death. This man with his sandy brown hair and chiseled features is the epitome of excellent health. His tailored black suit, which I picked up from the cleaners, only emphasizes the virile power in his tall frame.

"This isn't a top," he points out, staring at the oversized streusel muffin.

I hold up a finger, walk to my desk, and return with a pair of scissors.

Before he can object, I take the muffin and snip off the top.

"Now it is," I tell him, placing it on the delicate tissue wrapper.

He arches a brow before leaning back in his executive leather chair, and I hightail it out of his office before things escalate. By escalate, I mean him firing me.

When I sink down into my chair, my phone vibrates. I read the text message from my best friend, Julie:

"Did you pick a pen name?"

"Not yet," I reply back. "I might be scared."

There's no might, really— I'm terrified. If fright had a face, it would be mine. I've written lots of things but never put them out into the world. My phone vibrates again, this time with a call.

"Hey," I whisper, "what if he finds out? What if my family finds out? I used the words pussy and cock."

"Listen," she whispers back, "do you want to be an author or do you want to always wish you had?"

Julie is one of those types of people who is fearless. My hesitation is foreign to her. When I met her two years ago at my last job, it was a classic case of opposites attract. Introvert and extrovert. Sprinkle cupcake and plain vanilla. When I sat in on a meeting about marketing graphics, I was in awe of her periwinkle hair and diamond studded nose. When she wants something, there's no hesitation, no thinking it through for years like me. She wanted her own graphic design business—done. Just like that.

I drum my fingers on the desk. I know she's right. I don't want to always wonder what it would have felt like to publish because I was too scared to actually do it.

"Ok, let me think on the name."

"Rose, you've been thinking for a month; you're stalling. I just need a name to finish the cover. How about Ruby Red?"

Ruby Red. A little homage to my hair. The hair that's going to fall out from anxiety. "Ok, Ruby Red it is."

She squeals into the phone. "Give me two minutes, and I'll send it over."

We hang up, and true to her word, two minutes later, I'm staring at the *Love Doctor* cover in all its shirtless glory. Julie designs a lot of romance covers and assured me that abs is what sells. In the middle of wondering if Dr. Sincock's chest is etched like this marble god, I nearly jump out of my seat when his deep voice says, "You dropped this."

In his hand is a yellow note—*my* yellow note with 'angry sex' scrawled across it.

2

Declan

On average, doctors interrupt their patients during a consultation once every fourteen seconds. The busier a doctor tends to be, the more likely they are to interrupt.

I DON'T THINK Rose likes me very much. And I don't know why that thought bugs the hell out of me. She needs a desk plate that reads: Rose Thorne, Administrative Assistant, and a fucking thorn in my side.

What's not to like about me? I wouldn't say I'm a cocky guy —oh wait, can I say cocky?

Let's start over, I wouldn't say I'm an arrogant guy. I'm not haughty or conceited. I just know how to get things done, in the best possible way. Except, right now. Instead of preparing for my first client, angry sex is all I can think about. Angry sex with Rose.

Her cheeks flame the same rich hue as her hair when she takes the square piece of paper from my fingers. "Thanks," she says, balling the yellow paper into her fist and tossing it into the trash can, with no elaboration as to its meaning.

"Is that regarding a client?" I dig for info, knowing it's not. But, as a sex therapist, it's highly possible this could be related to one of my patients, so my question is valid, even if I'm only interested in how it pertains to Rose.

Wide-eyed, she tucks a stray strand of hair behind the shell of her ear. "Um, no."

Still no elaboration. Rooted to the marble floor, I slide my hands in my pockets. Obviously I can't ask her, because that would be unprofessional, so the right thing to do in this situation would be to just fucking tell me. You can't just drop a bomb like that and then not explain. I'm sure her silence is because she doesn't like me, and our lack of a copacetic working relationship is her fault, really. If she didn't walk around looking like sex on legs, I wouldn't have to send her out on errands, just so I can breathe. She's infuriatingly sexy. It's the fiery hair combined with dick stiffening glasses. I can't *not* look at her.

I don't like being attracted to my assistant, and I like even less she couldn't care less. And now I have to deal with this angry sex thing. A condom study I once read showed that women with red hair are more likely to be into bondage and kink. What exactly is she doing? And with who?

Again, she's a fucking thorn in my side.

What was I thinking hiring her?

I knew the moment she walked in, she was trouble. But I can't fire her now, and I sure as hell can't sleep with her. The only thing I can really do is boss her around, so I take great pride in that.

"Ok," I take another approach and perch on the edge of her desk, "is there something you'd like to talk about, Rose?"

Startled blue eyes lift from her computer screen. They are an arresting shade behind the black frames she sometimes wears, like someone took the raging sea and filled her iris.

"Not really," she says, a little dumbfounded at my question. "Thanks for asking."

"Ah. You sure?"

Her quieter than usual attitude is pricking my skin like a thousand needles.

Is it so hard to acknowledge my presence? Normally, I don't dwell on these things, but for some reason it irks me that she shuns me as if I'm a toxic virus.

She stands. "Positive. I have to run and make some copies before Mrs. Carter arrives."

Her vibrant red hair hustles past me. I probably stare a beat too long at the way her black slacks fondle her ass. There's no probably, I do. She's turning me into a human resource nightmare. I'd replace her if she weren't so damn efficient. I've never been so organized and horny in all my life. Well, fine. I don't need her to talk to me.

The rest of the morning, I stay sequestered in my office with Jacqueline Carter, a wealthy socialite who has a cheating husband. His philandering ways have diminished her sex drive to non existent. I listen as she takes the blame on herself for his affairs. The non professional part of me wants to tell her to find a man who can keep his dick in his pants, the professional part knows it's not that simple.

Sometimes I love what I do, other times, like now, I question my choice. When I first went into medical school, I had my whole career mapped out with the end result as a plastic surgeon. Since living in LA is a goldmine for surgeries in that field, easy choice.

Except, the Sun Valley is saturated with doctors who had the same thoughts as me, so I remapped my life and went where I was needed, where I could actually make a difference—in the bedroom. And it was great for a while, but now I feel like I could be doing more. I want more.

Once Jacqueline's session has ended, and I've finished my notes, I head outside for fresh air and cross the lot to my favorite once a week food truck: 'Wanna Taco Bout It.'

It's late, so the normal throng of employees waiting in line is nonexistent. Except, a lone redhead at the neon yellow truck's order window.

Rose.

"You know it's Thursday, right?" I say, stepping up behind her.

She turns to face me, taco in hand.

"Who says you have to only have tacos on Tuesday?"

"Same people who say you have to have pizza on Fridays."

She gives me a glimpse of a smile. "They just don't understand the Thursday craving for a taco."

"Exactly. They aren't true taco aficionados." I step up to the window and glance back at Rose. My eyes examine the glints of gold in her dazzling red hair, the graceful lines of her exposed neck, and the, well, I don't want to be that asshole guy objectifying women, but her breasts are stellar.

She turns away to grab a few napkins. "Are you here for a taco?"

"Are you offering me yours?"

She spins back around, and I can't help but focus on her upper lip line. According to a study in *The Journal of Sexual Medicine*, prominent upper lip tubercles indicate a woman's ability to have a vaginal orgasm. Ok, let me leave out the medical jargon —Rose's lips tell me she wouldn't need my finger on her clit to get her off.

Irritation grips my shoulders, knotting them, that I would even notice. That I want to test the theory.

"Well, no," she finally says, breathy and innocent.

Of course she wouldn't give me her taco. Not that I would take her taco, but I'm sure it's delicious. Furthermore, I will never know because Rose is my employee, not someone I can fuck and forget. I can already tell that about her. She'd claw her way in and spread until I was trapped in love soaked brambles, unable to break free from her intoxicating taste. And that just can't happen.

So, I step up to the window and order, because again, she's a fucking thorn in my side.

3

Rose

"Write what you know." —*Mark Twain*

I'M A HOT MESS. Was his question about my taco a euphemism? It's a little disturbing I wanted to scream 'yes, take my taco' and shove it all over his beautifully sculpted face.

When he confronted me about the angry sex note, I wanted to curl into a ball and roll away. How could I even explain to him the note? I couldn't exactly say, 'You drive me nuts, and I want to shove you against the wall and have angry sex.'

So I can obsess over him undetected, I find a secluded bench in the shaded courtyard to dine on my taco and watch as Declan talks to the guy working the truck. It's hard to believe a man like him is single. As far as I can tell from managing his life, he's not involved with anyone. Long term, anyway. He's so self assured, so composed as he lounges against the window counter without a care in the world. Like he has all day to stand there, talking to the man behind the counter. Lust emerges in a sheen of sweat between my breasts as I watch him. I've never had any man affect me in this way. Well, I haven't had many men, so there's that, but none of my previous boyfriends made me want to write about them. They were all very bland. Dry toast to his buttery croissant. They certainly never made my boobs perspire.

To avoid staring at him, I pull out my phone and plot a quick scene in my notes for *Love Doctor*. My romance book that started out as an homage to Declan, has turned into so much more with real, breathing characters I torture each day. I should probably abort this mission to publish a book loosely based on my boss, but I'm too attached to the characters. They won't stop flitting through my head.

When I'm done creating havoc for my heroine, Annette, I toss the remainder of my lunch in the trash and glance up to see Declan striding toward me with purpose until his black leather shoes stop right in front of my bench. Rather than give into my primal instinct to bolt, I slip my phone into my bag and meet his encompassing stare.

"I'd like to go over a few things with you after your lunch. Make a to do list for an upcoming trip I'm taking."

"Sure," I stand, "I'm on way back now. I'll meet you there."

"I'll walk with you."

"Ok."

We don't say a word to each other on the walk back inside, and that suits me just fine. His voice does things to me, so I'd rather not hear it right now. Thankfully, a small crowd of employees await the elevator, so I won't be alone with him.

We step into the elevator and I shuffle to position myself in the corner where it's safe. I need at least three arm lengths between us.

He's too fast, going for the same spot, and as I step back, my butt cheeks make contact with his groin in the crowded space. It feels like someone stuck an electrode to my ass. He must've felt it too, because what sounds like a whisper hiss sounds from his lips before his hand grips my hip. Dena, a tall blonde from accounting, blocks me from moving forward, so I tilt my pelvis forward a bit to no avail.

He releases me, and I'm grateful for the drone of polite elevator chatter to drown out the thunderous rhythm of my heart as the elevator ascends at an achingly slow pace.

After what seems like centuries, the lift dings and a few people vacate. And so do I. Out of my peripheral, I see the bewildered look on Declan's face as I exit, but I keep moving toward the door that leads to the stairs.

On the three remaining flights up to his floor, I compose myself as best I can now knowing that Dr. Sincock is indeed Dr. Bigcock. When I named the character Eclan Bigcock, it was sort of a joke, but um, yeah, he's packing. And if I'm not mistaken, he was semi hard.

As I approach, through the glass windows of the office, I see him standing by my desk. Mentally, I take a deep breath before opening the door.

"Just needed to work off that taco," I use as an excuse when I enter the office.

"Ah," is his only response, as if he knows exactly why I left.

"Where would you like me?" I ask, bending over to put my handbag in the bottom drawer of my desk. When I lean up, and turn, he's right there, and my breasts make contact with the steel muscles of his chest. He steps back as if I burned him with my nipples. And then he makes everything worse.

"I'll need you to accompany me on the trip." Before I can object, he stalks toward his office door. "I'll just email you the specifics."

The specifics, right. Hopefully, they'll include instructions on how to handle myself professionally with my boss for a trip out of town.

⌐⌐

"BAD DAY?" Julie texts in answer to my crying emoji I texted her as I sit parked in Christian's driveway for my weekly critique meeting.

"The worst." Not just a bad day, it's been a bad week, actually. Ever since Declan told me I'd have to accompany him to Santa Maria, things have been tense. Why does he need me there? All week long, I've tried to come up with a reason I can't go—fear of bridges, sudden food poisoning, cramps—but, unfortunately there isn't one that will work. And now, to add insult to injury, I have to sit through hours of sex scene shaming. "I'm not really looking forward to tonight," I confess.

"I thought you liked going?"

"I used to."

The writing critique group was so much fun when I first joined. Interacting with other authors made me feel as if I was actually moving toward my seemingly unattainable goal. But now, I just feel so out of place. I feel as though I'm moving backwards. The other writers have a formula they follow that doesn't fit into my vision of being a published author. I always pictured it as lazy days behind a desk, writing the words I want to write, not pumping the same old garbage out again and again. Is that so wrong? Are these people really the 'say all' in books?

"What's really going on?"

"Remember how Pru called my scenes tame? Well, maybe she's right, and it's because I'm not very sex savvy."

"Sex savvy?" She laughs a little. "You need to get laid."

"No, I don't."

"Yes, you do. Let's go out."

"I have my writing group to go to."

"I'll meet you after."

I'd much rather curl up on my couch and Netflix. It's easy to get caught up in my head and forget an outside world exists, because, in my mind, I've been so many places. Real life kind of sucks sometimes.

She finally convinces me and we make plans to meet at Patty's Pub after I'm done. Maybe she's right, and I need to get laid. Just let myself go and have sex with no commitment.

With dread, I grab my handbag and make the short trek up the drive to Christian's front door and knock.

He opens the door of his rambler-style home and welcomes me in. "The others will be here any minute," he informs me as I step inside.

We've had numerous meetings in Christian's home, and I still get goosebumps when I see the wall-to-wall bookshelves in his spacious living area. I love books. I just do. Everything about them—the smell, the feel, what's inside. Christian has enough books for his own library and every time I'm immediately drawn toward the floor-to-ceiling shelves.

"This is cool," I say, moving to check out his new design on the center shelf.

"I have them organized by color."

Every week he does something different. This week it's a mini rainbow. I smile, moving closer to inspect his handiwork.

The first book in the spectrum of colors is thick and red, and I run my finger down the spine. "Dracula. Good choice."

"It's a favorite."

There's a knock at the door and Christian turns away from me to answer. The voices of Rebecca and Pru sound from the entry, cutting short my book envy. Instead of the leather sofa, where I might get stuck next to Pru, I take a seat on a yellow wingback chair and grab a few bite-sized hor d'oeuvres from the tray on the coffee table, shoving them in my mouth so I won't have to make idle chit chat.

"Let's get started," Christian says, leading them into the living room. "Rose, why don't we start with you."

Pru and her ego take a seat on the couch across from me. "Yes, let's save the best for last," she jokes.

"You mean the one with the best ghostwriter," Rebecca mumbles, sitting in the chair beside me.

The cocktail wieners threaten to come up at the thought of sharing my work again. My short probably reads like a children's book next to theirs, and everyone will say the scene is still too tame, even though I used the word pussy—twice. Reluctantly, I pass out the printed copies of my five-hundred word fuckfest.

This time, to really stretch my writing flexibility, I went with vampire sex. In an elevator. Ugh.

The elevator doors swoosh closed and Eclan grabs me from behind, his fangs dangerously close to my neck.

"Your pulse is racing," he whispers, sweeping my hair off my shoulder. "Are you afraid or turned on?"

"Both."

My pussy aches with need, wanting more than anything for him to claim me right here. Right now.

His fangs prick my neck in a slow tease, just enough to barely puncture my soft skin. The searing pain is overshadowed by primal pleasure. He licks the love bite, and I brace my hand against the metal wall of the elevator, pushing my ass against him.

"Fuck me," I plead.

For a moment, I think he's going to deny me, until I hear the distinct sound of his zipper inching down. He's a master tease, brushing his dick against my ass. It's huge.

Chills fan across my skin when he runs his warm hand up my thigh to play with my pussy. I moan.

And then with a guttural growl, he ends the sweet agony, pounding inside me with vampiric force. My blood boils with desire. This is wrong, I tell myself.

But, my heart is too far gone to listen.

Christian's eyes meet mine as he places his paper on the coffee table. "Much better," he says, coughing a bit. "This isn't from the book you're working on, is it?"

I smile, feeling like I'm finally getting the hang of this sex stuff. Obviously, I'd love for people to take something meaningful away from my stories, feel that tug in their gut, but if I can turn people on from my writing, and they feel it in their vaginas, I'll take that too. "No, this was just a little scene I threw together."

My temporary high is short lived when Pru's critique brings me down to Earth. "I wouldn't touch myself," she says. "I think you need to get naughtier. Your sex scenes are not there yet. He should've fucked her in the ass. Maybe had his vampire buddies participating, watching in the mirror."

Pru is a best-selling author, and I should be honored she's even reading my scenes, but I'd be lying if I said her criticism wasn't getting on my last nerve.

If I were a confrontational type person, I'd tell her to shove a dick in her mouth, but I'm not. Instead, I save my animosity to be worked out between my characters. I blink and then finally find my words to respond. "Well he's huge, so they'd need lube. It kind of ruins the moment to pull out a big bottle of lube?"

Rebecca laughs. "Plus vampires don't have reflections."

"It's fiction," Pru shoots back. "They can do whatever they want."

"Well he doesn't like to share," I add. And neither do I. After all the scenes are read, Christian dismisses us, and I can't get to the bar fast enough.

The Irish pub is packed when I arrive and I squeeze through clusters of people until I find Julie in a booth by the stage. Her short black hair with periwinkle streaks is easy to spot in a crowd.

After a few drinks, some of the tension slips away. "I need sex scene help."

Julie chews on the black stirrer from her drink. Her brown eyes focus all on me. "Ask me. I know a few tricks."

I shake my head. "It isn't just tricks. I should write from my own experiences. Maybe you're right. Maybe I should have sex tonight." I'm so missionary position. It never even crossed my mind to go for anal in that scene, or ménage.

"Yes," Julie grins, nodding her head, "now you're talking." She swivels in her seat, taking in the whole place. "Let's see." She points to a man by the door in a black sweater and jeans. "How about him?"

"I didn't mean right now," I say with a laugh.

But, Julie ignores me. "Seriously, what about him?" She points to the same man again.

"Too short."

"Him." She points to his friend wearing a red Polo and khakis.

"Too tall." He is really tall, like *Jack and the Beanstalk* tall. I'd need a ladder to reach him.

"How about Doctor Sex?"

"Who?" I know exactly who she's referring to, although I pretend I don't.

"Dr. Bigcock."

I shush her. "You can't mention that name out loud." I glance around to be sure no one overheard.

"How's the book coming along? Aren't you excited?"

I shrug. "I'm not really sure." Maybe it would feel better if Julie wasn't the only person on the planet who knows I'm writing it. Since I can't share the news with friends and family, it's lackluster at best. It's like a celebration with no one there. Not to discount Julie, of course.

"Well, any plans on when you're releasing it?"

I laugh. "Maybe never."

"You can't not publish it," she chastises me before eating the olive from her martini. She points the toothpick at me. "People will love it. Believe me. And I've got connections who can help."

"I don't know." Despite all the knowledge Julie has bestowed on me from her experience designing covers for some of what she says are the hottest romance writers, I'm terrified.

"Wait." She fishes another olive out of her martini glass and pops it into her mouth. "You aren't letting your critique group read your book, are you?"

"No. I'm just doing little random scenes here and there for them."

She takes a sip of her drink. "Good, cause they steal ideas."

I grab my own drink. "I don't think anyone would want to

steal my ideas." And it's true. I'm not a noteworthy author or anything.

"Um," Julie points toward the door, "isn't that your boss?"

In an exorcist-like move, I twist my head and spot Declan walking into the club with a dark haired man. "I swear hot people hang out with hot people," she muses. "You really need to have sex with him. For me."

I finish off my Cosmo, taken aback by the sight of casual Declan in jeans and a black button down. "He's not really my type."

Julie's brown eyes narrow, calling out my lie. "Successful and gorgeous aren't your type?"

"He's my boss, that automatically makes him not my type." I watch them approach the bar where two leggy blondes set their sights on them. I'm sure he'll be all over them in no time and I don't want to stay to find out. "Let's go before he sees me."

"Wait," she gulps her martini down, "I'm not done drinking."

I grab her arm, moving her along the seat. "Great thing about this town is there's plenty of places to drink."

4

Declan

A study performed in the United States found that doctors who played video games on a regular basis made 37% less errors and were 27% faster than their non-gaming coworkers.

THIS IS DEPRESSING. Why I let Jonah, my brother-in-law, bring me to this miserable club, I'll never know. This is not my scene. A band plays a fast, upbeat song. Maybe I'm too tense. Maybe I should just go home and read, because this place isn't doing it for me. I can't relax.

Two women, wearing next to nothing, saunter up, batting their spider lashes in our direction.

Without being downright rude, Jonah flashes his wedding ring, tells them we're not interested, and they vanish with disappointment clear in their heavily made up faces.

"You weren't interested, right?" Jonah asks, his brown eyes shining with a hint of laughter.

I shake my head, smiling slightly. "Guess not." The truth is, I'm only interested in the splash of red catching my attention in the corner by the band. It almost looks like Rose. Almost.

This is becoming a real problem. I need to fuck Rose out of my system with someone else. When she beheaded my muffin, my first instinct was to bend her over my desk and spank her. That would probably cost me my license.

Jonah and I grab a beer and weave through the throng of people to a quieter room with pool tables.

I stare at his t-shirt with the words 'I eat cake because it's somebody's birthday somewhere' sprawled along the front, and laugh. "When are you going to grow up and get a real wardrobe?"

"Hey, don't knock the shirt. What's crawled up your ass?" Jonah asks, racking the balls.

"Got a lot on my mind." Like Rose. And how infuriating she is.

"Chelsea comes back into town on Friday, we should get some video game time in before she comes home."

Still feels weird that my sister is married to my best friend. When they fell in love, I wasn't too happy at first, but now, seeing how much he loves her, how he handles her movie star fame and keeps her grounded, I couldn't ask for a better husband for Chelsea.

"Sure, I'm always up for gaming," I agree. "Feels like forever since I spanked your ass in Call of Duty. Maybe Thursday. I'd have to check my schedule at the clinic."

"Are they paying you yet?" he asks about the clinic, leaning over the table to break.

"Nope. Still volunteer work." And I like it that way. The job at the low-income clinic downtown, where I volunteer a few weekends a month, isn't about money. It's probably the one thing that isn't.

He moves around the table. "How's the day job?"

"What are you writing a book?"

He knocks a solid ball into the corner pocket and shrugs. "Just asking."

"It would be better if I had an assistant who didn't drive me insane."

He looks up. "I thought you said she was working out great? The redhead, right?"

"Yeah."

He sinks another ball, then continues wiping the table clean with each shot. Ball after ball falls into each pocket around the table. Fuck.

"Looks like you won't be playing tonight," he smirks, leaning over the table and lining up his next shot.

"Lack of sex makes for a better pool player."

My remark does its job and the seven ball scoots around the corner pocket and stops. "Fuck you," he says, with a grin.

I laugh—even though I know all too well about lack of sex —taking my first shot and sinking lucky number thirteen. I haven't gotten laid in ages, which is probably why I'm hyper aware of the red-haired beauty who works for me.

Actually, I can't remember the last time I even dated anyone. Oh wait, I once went out with my sister's best friend, Gidget, which didn't work out. We had nothing in common. And besides, that was a long time ago.

We shoot pool for a few hours and then call it a night. On our way out of the club, Jonah turns to me. "Booker's been wanting us all to come up to Ferndale."

"That so?" I've been best friends with Jonah, Ethan, and Booker since we were kids, and we always manage to hang out whenever we can. But more often that not, lately, it seems I can't. I always feel like I'm so busy. So busy working. "Speak of the devil." I show my ringing phone with Booker's name to Jonah, and he laughs.

"Tell him I'll be coming up this weekend," Jonah says as I answer the phone.

"Hey, man." I step outside.

"Declan," Booker says, "we need a guy's weekend. You free?"

"It's your lucky day, I am." I'll have to double check my

schedule, but I need to make time for this. I'm stressed beyond belief and could use some time away with the guys.

"Awesome."

"How's Ferndale?"

"Great. You haven't been here since the wedding. I was starting to get offended."

"I've just been busy. Things good with Cat and Cooper?"

"They're both great. I actually just got done with the process of adopting Coop."

He fills me in on his wedded bliss. I can feel the love permeating through the phone for Cat and her son, defrosting my cold black heart just a tad. Maybe one ventricle. "It's late, what are you doing up?"

"Oh, that's a story for when I see you in person this weekend, my friend."

"I'll be there." I can already feel some of this tension slipping away.

A few days away from the siren in my office is exactly what I need.

⊏⊐

BOOKER ALWAYS SAYS RUNNING IS the best way to clear your head, and right now I need a clear fucking head. Summer sunlight pours through the wood blinds in my living room, shining along the hardwood floors as I lace my sneakers. I stand and roll my neck to the side, raising an arm above my head, letting the muscles stretch completely. This is out of routine for me. I always start my mornings the same way—coffee, shower, work. I've become a mundane creature of habit who is accustomed to having things the way I like them. Georgia, my housekeeper, says I need a woman in this big house. I like not having to worry about anyone touching my collection of old medical journals—and yes, it's an extensive collection, sprawling from

the bookshelves in my office into the shelves in my living room
—or planning my day with nonsense.

I like the sanctity of my own home, of my own personal
space, but this place almost feels hollow to me. Like, I need a
change, and a drastic one.

When I took the sex therapist job, it was always thought of
as a temporary fix. Something to tide me over until I landed the
dream job.

But then, time passed and I stayed stuck in the job I never
really wanted, making money I barely have time to spend.

I walk into the kitchen to grab a bottle of water before my
run. I've never liked running, and here's why—running
sucks ass.

Putting one foot in front of the other, exerting all of your
energy, using every muscle, having nothing to focus on but the
road...it's exhausting and horrible.

But, I need a clear head. So, today is the day I will try this
running business to see if it's for me.

I take a deep breath, open my front door, and step out into
the fresh air of Cali. (there's a little smog, sure.)

In my driveway, I stretch my legs, bouncing around a little to
warm up, and then start off in a slow jog. I try to let the peace
and quiet of the early morning drown out the loud thoughts
circulating in my mind. Like a ghost haunting me, Rose refuses
to let that happen. What was that angry sex note all about?
Does she have a boyfriend? Was that note meant for some type
of what's to come between them?

I pick up the pace, my sneakers pounding the pavement, as I
try desperately not to think about angry sex with Rose and her
long red hair twisted around my fist, me thrusting into her at a
thundering speed, her moans loud enough for the whole world
to hear them.

Running with a semi is never a good thing, so I come to a
dead stop on the corner of my neighborhood, and bend over to
deal with my hyperpnea. Basically, I'm gasping for air.

Sure, I've had a sort of thing for my assistant for way too long, but seeing the angry note made it a million times worse. It made the purely innocent thoughts I was having about her turn into naughty X-rated versions of the porn variety type thoughts.

And what makes it worse, I still have no idea why that note was even written.

When I can breathe, I start up my jog again, wondering why anyone on this earth would ever do this for fun. I scan the neighborhood, and I've barely even gone a block. So, I pick up the pace once more, letting thoughts of saving lives, curing diseases, and actually helping people enter my head instead.

The pavement blurs as my slow jog turns into a full-on sprint and I try desperately to release the tension building between my shoulder blades.

I read a study once in a medical journal that says running releases endorphins which make you happy. It said they're structurally the same as morphine, so it's nature's painkiller, causing euphoria and an overall sense of general well-being. Yeah, that's bullshit. My receptors must be broken.

Because as I slow down and walk the rest of the way back to my house, I am not happy. Nor do I have a clear head. I guess one could say I was trying to metaphorically run away from my problems. That problem being Rose. And they'd be right.

5

Rose

"And by the way, everything in life is writable about if you have the outgoing guts to do it, and the imagination to improvise. The worst enemy to creativity is self-doubt."

— *Sylvia Plath*

"THOSE MUFFINS ARE no longer the same," my father's deep voice booms across the packed auditorium. "You have to follow *His* recipe."

I squirm a bit in my padded black seat, tugging at the hemline of my chaste navy dress while he glides across the oval stage as if he's walking on water, going on about not tainting your muffin. The adoring camera zooms in on his charismatic suited figure, and he smiles for the viewers watching from the comfort of their living rooms, driving whatever message he's preaching about home. It works, because I feel like a little girl again being chastised for not cleaning my room. Not that I was a rebellious child, quite the opposite. Dutiful, I guess would be a good word.

"Keep the muffin pure," Dad sort of whisper advises for full effect.

I never should've agreed to come today. I should've stayed home and reassessed my life goals. Guilt is a powerful thing, though. Powerful enough for me to wake at six am on a Sunday and file into this auditorium filled with hundreds of people just to make my father happy. It's not powerful enough, however, to keep me from zoning out and missing whatever this muffin talk was about. There's no way he could know what I did, but ironic my father chose to speak to his flock about muffins after my incident with Dr. Sincock. I shake my head, trying my best to erase the naughty, sinful thoughts I'm having about Sincock. Ugh, just his name. Sin-cock.

And what a beautifully sinful cock it probably is.

Oh God. Stop taking the Lord's name in vein. Vain.

I snap my head up to the front of the church.

I will not have impure thoughts about my boss while listening to my father's sermon. My father's always had that ability to make me think he knows what I'm doing, which in turn, ensured I didn't do anything. I mean, for Christ's sake—forgive me, Jesus—I'm a grown woman hiding my true passion. My writing about cocks would most definitely be frowned upon by Gregory and Molly Thorne. Well Gregory, anyway. Mom always did the best she could in the situation, giving me just enough leash to experience life without fully experiencing it. Well, today just might be the day I confess and everyone can just deal.

All that courage dissipates the moment the sermon is over and I sit down to brunch with my parents and don't tell them about my novel.

"How's work, Rose?" my dad asks, slicing through his Eggs Benedict. "Remind me what type of doctor you're working for now?"

I chew my bacon until there's nothing left to swallow. I'm sure that's another thing that would be frowned upon, my working for a sex therapist. This is why I don't do sit downs very often. Even though I'm an adult, free to make my own choices, I'm conditioned to not make them without their approval.

"A therapist," I answer.

"That sounds interesting," Mom adds. "You like him?"

"It's just temporary," I answer, avoiding the question.

Dad's face pulls down into a frown. "If you need a job, my offer still stands."

"I'm good, Dad." He's never been happy with my decision to not work in his empire. *Grace with Gregory* pulls in big numbers —viewers and dollars. But that's his dream, not mine. My dream is never going to happen, if I don't make it happen.

Mom intercedes and gracefully changes the subject like a pro.

After we finish, I head back to my apartment with new resolve to publish my novel. Once inside, I change into cotton shorts and a baggy T-shirt and sit down at my desk to write.

For inspiration, I pull up the cover Julie designed and sit in silence, listening to the clock tick on the bookshelf in my living room. This is part of my relationship with writing. This is how I operate. Some people listen to music, I need quiet. It's tricky straddling the line between fiction and reality. Men like this don't exist in real life. Like the alpha male who will go to Hell and back to protect his woman and makes her orgasm by just a simple command.

Thoughts spin their way through my mind, weaving words together, and my fingers fly over the keyboard. My inner thoughts pour out of me. After a long while, I lose my mojo and my sleep-deprived eyes can't focus any longer. There's so much more about Annette I want to get out onto the pages.

Many people say you write what you know, that your charac-ters wear a few of your qualities in their souls. That's true; Annette is a lot like me. She's also a lot of the things I wish I could be.

I read through what I've written, making sure to save everything, and then head off to bed, trying not to think about whether what I just wrote is too tame. I need a neutral party to read it. An idea forms in my overtired brain, when I slide under the covers. It may be a lousy one, or it could be the most brilliant idea I've ever had. Maybe it isn't the advice of other writers I need to be seeking, but an actual expert in the field. Someone like Dr. Sincock. If anyone knows sex, it's him.

WHEN I ENTER Declan's office the next morning with his coffee, he doesn't look up from whatever he's wrapped up in on his phone. I slide the mug on his desk, peeking under my lashes at the deep in thought look on his handsome face.

"Can I ask you something?"

He looks a little startled by my question. Normally we don't speak at the coffee drop off, so this is highly unusual. "Sure," he finally answers.

I slide my phone out of my pocket. "Can you read this? My friend needs advice and well, you're the expert."

"What is it?"

"It's a little sex scene." He doesn't blink. "My friend wrote it." I feel like he's not believing my lie, so I add, "Her name is Julie and she sometimes writes."

He raises a brow before looking down at my phone, reading aloud, "'He's the type of man who wants what he wants with no thought to the ripple effects of his actions. He's delicious but so is cake.'"

The sound of my words from *Love Doctor* coming out of his mouth sets my heart slamming against the shield of my chest. This was a dumb idea. I hope he remembers his medical training, because I'm going to need CPR. Everything in the room blurs, closing in on me. Annette had a moment like I'm experiencing, and I realize I did a horrible job with the visual.

He goes silent as he continues reading the sensual scene. At least, I hope it's sensual. His green eyes impale me, when he's done reading.

Composing myself, I slip my sweaty palms into the pockets of my slacks. "Is it hot?" I lick my suddenly parched lips and reach down for his untouched coffee and take a sip before my throat closes. He's going to have to do one of those pen stab things to my neck to let some air in.

"Are you ok?" His eyes track the movement of my hand as I set his mug back down.

"Yes. So, what do you think?" And then I give in to my basic instincts and ask what I shouldn't. "Too tame?"

"Eh, yeah, it's a little on the tame side. Very mild."

"Thanks, I'll let her know." What the hell are people doing that I'm not aware of? "Is there anything else you need?"

"Yes, actually," he answers, switching back to employer mode. "I'm visiting a friend in Ferndale and need you to schedule a flight and a rental car. I'll send you the days."

"Perfect." My smile I give him before I turn to leave belies the fact I'm actually a little bit hurt. I don't like this feeling. Logically, I know I need armadillo skin if I'm going to survive, but right now, it's tissue paper. And he just unknowingly shredded it.

6

Declan

Doctors have a short temper. This is fiction not fact.

I'M NOT A PATIENT MAN. Nor am I the size of an elf. I stare at the matchbox-sized white Scion waiting for me at the airport. It looks like someone rammed it against a concrete wall—front and back—it's ridiculous. I send a text to Rose: *Where is the rest of my car?*

A few minutes later she replies: *Too tame for you? Think of all the environment you're saving. It gets great gas mileage.*

She's always doing these types of things to get under my skin, which is another reason I'm positive she must hate me. I'm sure with all that pent up anger, it would be an epic hate fuck.

I shovel my frame into the car the size of a peanut. Surprisingly it's roomier than expected, but not by much.

Once I figure out how to drive this thing, I hit the road. Being in Ferndale, California is like traveling back in time. It's got that Mayberry feel tossed with the granola-crunchers of the Northwest. Hidden in the depths of the Redwoods, and backing up to the Pacific Ocean, it's paradise. I can see why Booker picked this place to raise his family, because nowhere else in the country I've seen offers magic like this place does.

When I pull into Booker's driveway, Jonah and Ethan are already here. The guys wait for me on the porch, laughing as I try desperately to get out of the Scion contraption.

"What happened to your car?" Booker asks with a smirk, his dark eyes surveying the mini rental.

"My assistant, Rose, set it up for me." I grab my bags from the trunk and set them down to give each of the guys a handshake.

"You must have pissed her off pretty bad," Ethan surmises as we head toward the front door of Booker's two-story Victorian home.

I shrug as we enter. "Guess she's resistant to my charm."

He may be right, but I can't think of a thing I could have done to set her off. What did I do to make her *this* upset?

As soon as Booker shuts the door, his wife, Cat, waggles her eyebrows at me as she rounds the corner. "Who could resist your charm?"

I give her a hug. "Just an assistant who hates my guts."

Cat smiles. "She probably doesn't hate you that much."

I give a slight eye-roll. "Doubt it. She *hates* me."

"She hasn't quit yet. Must not hate you too bad."

We head into the kitchen where Cooper sits eating Cheerios. Things have changed since I was here last. New granite countertops, peninsula, prep island, and new cabinets in a dark cherry-oak. It makes me feel a little guilty that I missed it.

"You got big," I say to Cooper, sitting at the center island.

"I'm ten-years-old, it would be expected."

Booker ruffles a hand through his sandy-brown hair. "Say hi," he instructs Cooper.

"Hi, Mr. Declan," Cooper complies through a mouthful of Cheerios.

Booker laughs. "It's *Dr.* Declan."

I hold up a hand with a smile. "Declan is just fine."

We all chat and catch up for a bit, and when Cat leaves the room, taking Cooper with her, I raise a brow at Booker. "I think I should be the one to address the issue we're all thinking," I start.

Jonah chuckles, lounging back against the countertop. "Yes, tell him."

Booker crosses his arm against his chest. "Tell me what?"

"While we're here, none of your naked morning rituals. We don't need to see that shit," Ethan finishes off for me.

Booker laughs. "I haven't done that since Cat and Cooper moved in."

"So, what's this big news?" Ethan asks Booker, changing the subject. He looks over at me. "He made us wait until you got here to tell us."

Booker's face lights brighter than the sun. "Cat's pregnant."

A round of congratulations ensue, and Booker looks ten years younger, like his jaded past is just that—the past.

He opens the fridge and tosses us each a beer.

I slap Booker on the shoulder before I take a seat at the island. "Congrats again, man. You deserve to be happy."

He nods in my direction. "So, do you. When are you going to settle down and have a few of your own?"

"Not anytime soon. I'm just so busy all the time."

"Can't be that busy. You found time to come here." He pops the top to his beer and takes a long pull.

"What's up with the assistant?" Booker asks. "What's her name?"

"Rose Thorne, and who knows. Did I tell you she murdered my muffin?"

Ethan nearly chokes on his beer as I tell them the story of Rose and all the things she does to annoy me.

"Sounds like foreplay," Ethan suggests, cocking a brow at me.

"She works for me," I dismiss the allegation. "Just because

you're in love with your stepsister, doesn't mean the rest of us cross the lines," I tease.

He gives me the finger, and I laugh.

"Do you need my love advice?" Booker jokes. "You can write the website if you want to remain anonymous."

"Such fucking comedians you all are." I smile. "Enough about Rose. What's going on with you guys?"

Booker spends the next few minutes filling us in on Cat and the pregnancy. When he called late the other night, it was because Cat isn't handling being pregnant very well. Instead of morning sickness, Booker tells us it's more like all-day sickness. His love advice website is booming with traffic and he's thinking about turning it into a vlog.

"I'd love to have you on the show sometime," he says.

"Anytime, just let me know when." I look over at Ethan. "How's Nova?"

"She's still as feisty as ever."

I take a pull of my beer listening as he tells us about traveling with Nova so she can use the experiences as segments on her show, 'The Fun Girl.' I never thought I'd see the day that Ethan Hale, bad boy movie star, would fall in love. But, then again, Nova is no ordinary woman.

"Actually, as soon as Nova is done filming, I go back into the studios to film a movie with Chelsea." Ethan waggles his eyebrows at Jonah, then at me.

"Are you love interests?" I ask, shocked that Jonah would ever be ok with this. It's bad enough when I found out Jonah was dating my sister, but now learning Ethan might be her love interest in a movie makes all the sick feelings come back.

"Over my dead body," Jonah says and Ethan bursts out with laughter.

I let out a deep breath. "I was worried there for a second. Bad enough I have to see Chelsea kiss this asshole," I point at Jonah. "But, having to see her kiss you would be worse."

Ethan holds a hand over his heart. "I'm hurt you would feel

that way. But, no. Chelsea and I actually play brother and sister in the movie."

"As her real life brother, I feel sorry for your character," I say before taking a swig from my Heineken.

"I heard that Declan," Cat chastises, walking in the kitchen, "and I'm going to call Chelsea and tell her what you said." Her blue eyes shine with humor.

We congratulate Cat on her pregnancy, and I stand to pull her in for a hug, asking her how far along she is and if she's taking her prenatals. A true doctor at heart.

Later in the evening, when we're getting ready to go out for dinner, I can't help but think about something Cat said about Rose. She said Rose hasn't quit yet, and the thought gnaws at me. The fact she hasn't quit means she's happy at her job. Either that or she needs the money bad enough to work for someone she hates. But, I don't think it's that. I think somewhere, deep down, she enjoys working for me. She must like me a little bit. Maybe I could be a little bit nicer. Maybe these gentler thoughts I'm having about Rose are all the side effects of having three faces of love staring at me all day. I perch on the edge of the bed in my room and send her a text to test the theory.

"Everything go ok in the office?"

I start small, nice and neutral. A few seconds later she replies. "Yes, very quiet. Tame, actually."

Now what? I can't ask her what she's wearing, although I'd really like to know, so I stay neutral.

"If you need anything, let me know."

"You do the same."

I swear she does these things to irritate me. Where's the exclamation point, an emoji, anything at all? I stand and slide my phone in my pocket. Cat is wrong, she definitely hates me.

⊏⎯⎯⊐

THE NEXT MORNING, the guys and I head off to the nearest

golf course under a clear blue sky. I'm glad I came on this trip. It's been too long since I've hung out with all the guys together. After we've finished the round of golf, we head to the members only bar inside and take a seat.

"How do you feel about becoming a dad, Booker?" Ethan asks, popping a few peanuts into his mouth.

The bartender slides Booker a Stella Artois, and Booker takes a long pull before answering, "Actually, I'm pretty fucking stoked."

"That's pretty cool." Ethan pulls a black jewelry box from his pants. "I'm going to ask Nova to marry me." He opens it, showing us all the square cut diamond inside.

"Dude, why are you carrying it around with you?" Jonah asks.

"I'm not letting this puppy out of my sight," he answers back.

I laugh. "You sure she'll say yes?"

He shoots me a death glare. "Of course she will." A look of panic crosses his face. "At least she'd better."

"I'm sure she will," Jonah adds, looking at the bartender. *"Martini. Gin, not vodka. Obviously. Stirred for ten seconds while looking at an unopened bottle of Vermouth."*

The guy behind the bar stares blankly at Jonah, unsure of what drink to actually make him.

"He's a movie savant," I say. "Just ignore him and give him a beer."

Jonah laughs. "Sorry, I'll take a Stella too."

The bartender bends to grab his beer from the cooler, and pops the top off. He hands it over to Jonah with a smile.

"He's probably quoting some movie no one has ever seen," Ethan adds, grabbing the bartender's attention.

"Oh shit, you're…"

Ethan smiles. "The one and only."

But the bartender isn't listening, he's shoving a scrap of

paper at Ethan, asking for an autograph. Ethan's cool with it, and he passes Ethan a pen across the oak bar.

"Everyone's seen Kingsman," Jonah adds as Ethan scribbles his name onto the white slip of paper for the bartender.

"Never heard of it," Booker says.

I tap my beer bottle with Booker in a cheers. "Me neither."

"Did you say your assistant's last name is Thorne?" Jonah asks, changing the subject. "Rose Thorne, right?"

"Yeah."

"Isn't her dad that guy on the TV?"

"What guy?" Ethan is very interested.

"The one...the preacher dude," Jonah adds.

Booker and Ethan laugh.

"No way." I'd know this fact. I did a thorough interview, and this is something that wouldn't have slid past me. Not that it really matters, and it wouldn't have affected me hiring her, but I would just know if her father was a famous preacher.

"Yes, Grace with Greg. Or something like that. He preaches about honesty and such." Jonah grabs his water bottle and takes a swallow before continuing, "Gregory Thorne? I think that's his name. I photographed him once and he mentioned his daughter—Rose."

I grab my phone from my back pocket. "Siri, who is Gregory Thorne?" The search pulls up images of a man behind a podium, preaching to the masses. I pull up a few of the sites, searching for any mention of a daughter. "Are you sure?"

"Pretty sure." Jonah and the guys stop what they're doing and peer over my shoulder, trying to get a better look at my phone.

I can't believe she never told me this. I can't believe I have to find this out from my own brother-in-law.

But, there she is, in color, sitting next to a woman with a red bob, and the caption reads, 'Wife and daughter to Gregory Thorne sit in the audience.'

I guess I don't know her as well as I thought I did. And that makes me sort of angry. Like I should know all the things about her but I don't.

My head is pounding, like someone beat it with a sledge-hammer. It's not like it's a big deal, and I'm not quite sure why I'm having a hard time with it. Is it possibly the fact I don't like someone else knowing something about my girl that I don't know? Not my girl, but my assistant. You know what I mean.

There's this whole new side to her I haven't quite figured out, and now all my thoughts are once again centered on her for the remainder of the trip. On the ride back to the airport the next morning— in my toy car—I can't help but wonder what else I don't know about this woman.

When I'm back to the office on Monday morning, I try to control my wicked thoughts when I see her now that I know she's a holy woman. I give her a good morning and stalk into my office and check over my schedule for the day. I have one new client scheduled early, and I let Rose know I'm ready.

I sit back, staring at all the degrees hanging on my wall, waiting for my next client to walk in.

And when she does, I realize I'm not ready at all.

7

Rose

"Every secret of a writer's soul, every experience of his life, every quality of his mind, is written large in his works."
— *Virginia Woolf*

ART IS SACRIFICE. So I'm sacrificing my lunch hour and two hundred dollars for some insight on sex. I've thought about it, and I have to break the barriers of my comfort zone in order to make myself better. This is my very own plot twist. Or this will be when Dr. Sincock fires me.

"Did my client cancel?" he asks, puzzled, as I cross to the leather chair in front of his desk.

"No," I take a seat, "it's me. Hi."

His brows draw together. "Um, what do you mean? Hi."

I know this is insane, and far outside the realm of employer/employee boundaries, but after giving it some thought, I've realized he's right. My book *is* tame. I'm tame. These characters are an extension of me and my experiences. The emotions and personalities flow freely, but when it gets to the sexy parts, it's lackluster. I've dwelled on his casual comment since he said it.

Renting him a miniature car was satisfying but doesn't fix how right he is. In order to make my book better, I have to take constructive criticism, and I need Dr. Sincock's expertise. Without him knowing, of course.

"Well," I cross my legs, settling back against the padded chair, "I've lead a somewhat sheltered life, and I've realized it's affected me in certain... aspects."

And it has. Sadly, that statement is not a manipulation of the truth.

"Rose," he gives a little disbelieving shake to his head, "are you wanting me to counsel you on sex?"

"Well, not like that," I hedge. It's a hundred degrees in here. Even the backs of my knees are sweating.

"Like what then?" he asks, leaning forward to rest his forearms on the desk, interlocking his fingers together.

I really have no idea what sex therapy entails. I look at the clock ticking away above his head. Five minutes already gone of my hour. "I can't orgasm during sex," I blurt out.

"Oh my god, Rose," he blurts back, standing. "You can't tell me these things."

"Why? You're a doctor, and I'm in need of help," I appeal to his suited back since he's now facing away from me, gazing out the window. Obviously, I could search the web, watch porn, or read something, but that's like hearing about someone else's cookie and trying to recreate it. Unless I know the actual recipe, or how the cookie tastes, I can't really paint a picture of how delicious it was. I can't make the reader feel what I felt. Which hasn't been a lot. Maybe I'm frigid.

He turns to face me. "There are other therapists."

"I can't just go to anyone." I meet his gaze. "I wouldn't feel comfortable."

"This would be highly unusual," he tells me, taking a seat again behind his desk, his face a complete mask of what he's possibly thinking about my request.

"That's not a no." Desperation to not fail drags me from my

chair to stand in front of his desk. "I'm just hoping maybe you can give me a few pointers." His face still gives nothing away. Maybe he's in shock. I should leave now, but instead I blurt out, "Maybe you can just give me one."

I think I crossed a line. Well actually, I know I did. I just asked my boss to get me off.

He laughs, but it's fake. As fake as the orgasms I pretended to have with my previous lovers. "Rose, that's not how sex therapy works."

"Right, I know. I didn't mean that," I lie, because I want to die of embarrassment. "Just say yes, please."

8

Declan

The majority of doctors consistently report working overtime.

I'VE NEVER CROSSED the boundaries of patient to doctor, ever. The line has always been drawn with a bold permanent marker, but for some reason Rose blurs that line for me.

It's as if she drew it in chalk, and it's a single raindrop from washing away. Raking a hand through my hair, I try to get a handle on the situation. A reason to justify agreeing to what she's asking of me. This is perfectly normal, isn't it? People come to me all the time for advice and therapy. I've always been the voice of reason for my friends, the sounding board for everyone close to me. I'm a professional, so I can do this.

"Let's consider this a consultation." Her shoulders slump with relief. "Have a seat, and I'll just ask some routine questions." I start with the obvious. "Are you sexually active?" God, please say no.

Her cheeks flush, and she glances down for a second at her nails. "Yes."

"You're lying."

Her eyes shoot up to mine. "No, I'm not."

I lean back in my seat. "Yes, you are." All my years of doing this has made me in tune when someone isn't being completely honest. Rose is definitely fibbing. I'm both elated and curious as to why she isn't having sex.

I stand, turning my back on her to stare out the window, pulling at my collar. Is it hot in here? "Are you dating?"

"No." I turn to face her and she stands. "This was a mistake." She rushes to leave, and I take a few steps to stop her at the door. "I shouldn't have thought this was a good idea."

I place my hand over hers on the handle of the door. "It is a bad idea." Our eyes meet. "Sit down," I tell her, against my better judgement.

She crosses the room back to her chair.

"It's just that…" her words fall away on a whisper.

I perch on the edge of my desk, facing her. "Let's start over. Tell me what's going on, Rose?"

She bites her bottom lip before answering. "I'm just not very...experienced. And I want to start having lots of sex."

I grip the edge of my desk, but continue as if that statement doesn't irritate me. "How many partners have you had?"

"Two."

Two. Two very lucky bastards who obviously didn't know what they were doing if they didn't make her come. I'll get through this session if it fucking kills me. "Well, intimacy and sex are nothing to be ashamed of. The two should go hand in hand. And it's perfectly natural to want to please your partner." I'm on autopilot. I sound like a high school guidance counselor, next thing I know I'll be telling her to make sure she's being safe.

"I do want to please them."

From knowing Rose the few months I have, I can tell she's a people pleaser. Which isn't a bad thing. And I have no doubt in my mind she'd be fantastic in bed. I mean, she'd please her partner just fine.

For fuck's sake. I scrub a hand down my face. "Why don't you tell me what the problem is?"

"Well, I've never had an orgasm from sex."

"But on your own you have? What about from oral?"

Oral is my specialty, I want to add. She shakes her head. "On my own, I'm a pro," Oh fuck, "but I've never had one with anyone else's help."

Ah, so it's not a medical problem. My guess is a wrong partner problem. I sit back down in my chair, my eyes having a hard time focusing on her. "I see."

All I see right now is my head between her legs, showing her what it feels like to come so hard she can't walk. I take a peek at the clock on the wall, watching each second tick by; this is the longest hour in history.

"I just want to know what that would be like," she continues the torture. "I want to know how to let myself go with a man."

I accept. I want to shout those words, and for some insane reason, I want to be the man she lets go with.

"And you think I can help?" I raise a brow.

"Yes, I think I just need some unorthodox treatment."

"Unorthodox how?"

"Well," she shifts in her chair, "I think maybe we could go over a few things. Like mechanics."

"You want me to teach you how to have sex?" I ask, bounding from my chair once again like a five-year-old who can't sit still. "This is insane, Rose."

Completely insane.

She shifts in her seat. "I know it's unusual. But, I figure you're the best person to come to for advice like this."

I take in a deep breath and let it out slowly. Think calming ocean. Think crashing waves. I glance at the clock, and she still has a little over half an hour. I yank at my blue tie.

Where do I fucking begin with this girl?

"I thought maybe you could suggest different …" her words

trail off, and I'm hanging on the edge of my seat trying to figure out what she wants me to suggest.

"Go on," I say when she doesn't continue.

"I just thought maybe you could offer different techniques. Maybe I'm doing something wrong?"

I hold up my hand, stopping her train of thought. "Rose, stop right there. It's not you, and I don't want you ever thinking that. Your partner should be fully invested in getting you to climax."

The sun rushes through the window, highlighting her flawless skin. I like the sun on her. She's probably only ever been with men who care about getting their own little rods off before they even have her fully turned on. Basically, she's probably only ever been with chumps. That thought pisses me off for some reason. Like I have to make it all better for her. Like I need to be the man of the hour and be the one to get her to come all over the place.

Fuck. Finally her hour is up.

"I understand if this is too weird," she says, pushing up from her chair. "Just know, I need help. I can find another sexpert, if you prefer."

Fuck that. "I'll have to think about this."

She nods. "Thank you. Your next client will be here in ten minutes."

And with that, she shuts the door, leaving me wondering what the hell to do. Another doctor helping her is probably best, mainly because she's too tempting, but whether I do the right thing remains to be seen, mainly because she's too fucking tempting.

⸻

YOU KNOW what's cool about living in LA? Famous people. You know what's cool about being related to a movie star? Nothing. I joke. My sister is still the same Chelsea she was before she shot to stardom. Corny jokes and all.

Want to go to a party tonight filled with sexy single women? her text reads. *Get it? Sexy...you're a sex therapist.*

I cringe a little. *Please stop. Your jokes are getting worse.*

You know you laughed.

No, I really didn't.

Mhm. So you interested? I can't make it, but thought you might be interested.

I don't even have to think about it. Being in the limelight is great for Chelsea and Jonah, and now for Ethan, too, but it's not for me.

I like the normalcy of grabbing a drink at the local bar and not being hounded for autographs of the people in my inner circle. Partying with the rich and famous was cool in the beginning, but after a few years, it fell flat. I wanted more out of life.

Nah, I'm good. Working at the Clinic.

Oh, that's right. Save lives, big bro.

I slide my phone back into the pocket of my slacks, lock up the house, and head off in the direction of downtown.

A few times a month, I put this medical license to good use and volunteer down at the free clinic on San Pedro Street. It's the least I can do, and it actually makes me feel like I'm doing something of value.

Sure, sex is an important part of any healthy relationship, but sometimes I feel like it's a shallow job. It's not what my passion is. I want to know I'm saving lives, does that make sense?

I pull into the back lot behind the brick medical building and grab my bag containing my stethoscope and white lab coat. It feels good to be here, and when I step inside, I get that rush like someone took a syringe and injected my veins with pure adrenaline.

"Hey, Hallie," I greet the nurse on duty, stepping behind the triage station.

"Dr. Sincock, hey. We have a full house tonight."

I grab the first chart in line. "That's how I like it." I step into the waiting room, studying all the faces in blue chairs, waiting to be seen. Hallie's right, this place is packed.

Over the baby cries, coughs, and cacophony of sickness I call out for Thomas Gibson.

A stout man with black hair, holding his arm, stands from near the back of the room. His tired face looks relieved, like he's been waiting in this room all day, and most likely he has.

"How are you doing today, Mr. Gibson?" I ask.

"Not too good. Hurt my arm."

He follows me down a short hallway into a small box of an exam room.

This clinic is cramped, and sometimes I wish I could buy the place, tear it down, and rebuild it bigger and stronger.

Mr. Gibson takes a seat in a small blue chair next to my computer station. With a click of the mouse, I bring up all the information I need to collect from him.

"Any allergies?" I ask. He shakes his head no and after I've gathered all his past history, I stand to check out his arm for swelling and tenderness. "How did you hurt it?"

"Helping my brother fix his truck. I don't really know how it happened. One minute it was fine, then the next it hurt."

"Let's get you x-rayed." I walk him down the hall to Radiology and ten minutes later my suspicions are confirmed.

"Well, your shoulder is dislocated. Did you fall?"

"No."

I raise a brow. "We can snap this back in. No fall?"

"My brother and I were fighting a bit."

"Ah, that explains it." I motion for Mr. Gibson to lie down on the exam table. "This might hurt a little."

Once I have his shoulder back in place, Mr. Gibson sits up and rotates his shoulder a few times. "Feels much better."

"Keep it immobile. Just go home, relax, and take some ibuprofen."

"Thank you, Doctor."

I walk him out, giving him further instructions on after care. When I get to the front, I make sure Hallie hooks him up with a sling.

The rest of the night passes swiftly, adrenaline carrying me throughout the rest of the evening. This is my element. This is what I should be doing. So much better than a party any day.

When I leave the clinic, I decide to take a walk downtown before heading home and dip into a little diner for a cup of coffee. I'm dead tired, but this feeling is something I miss from my time working a rotation in the emergency room.

The lights. The thrill of saving a life. The feeling of knowing you're making a difference in the world.

I stare into my coffee cup, watching the black liquid form swirls as I blow onto it.

A flash of red passes by the floor-to-ceiling windows of the restaurant, and I immediately think of Rose and wonder how she's spending her night.

Maybe she's on a date, with one of the men she needs sexual advice for. Anger courses through my system, and I try to push the thoughts away, but like a lingering guest, they won't leave. Like she's fastened herself into my system. The smart thing to do would be to not help her, but maybe it's best I face this head on. Sometimes the more you're around someone, the less attractive they become. Something tells me, that won't be the case.

9

Rose

"There is no greater agony than bearing an untold story inside you."
— *Maya Angelou*

MY CLOSET LOOKS like it belongs to Mother Teresa. All I need is a nun's veil for my head. It must be a subconscious result of my religious upbringing. Funny how we don't realize seeds are being planted in our brains until one day you see the forest. To play devil's advocate, I could also be boring.

The plastic hangers slide along the rail as I rummage through the colorful collection of business attire, looking for anything that will show off the girls. And I'd like to say, I truly must be a saint, because I don't have anything revealing. So many cardigans.

A black pencil skirt and white blouse make the cut today for work. I unbutton the top three buttons exposing the swell of my breasts, but it doesn't feel right. So, I button one back up and dab on a little mascara and gloss. Voila; I look like I'm going to church instead of tempting Dr. Sincock into helping me.

Deep breath.

I don't even know how to face him, I really don't.

But face him I will. On the way to work, I repeat that over and over in my head, so I don't turn around and go home. When I arrive at my desk, I'm immediately summoned into Declan's office.

Seriously, what was I thinking coming in today? Full of trepidation, I enter his office trying to get a feel for how bad I've messed things up. He looks troubled; that's not a good sign. His sandy hair, usually so perfect, looks like he's raked his hand through it a million times. Even his stern black suit looks like a bad omen.

He snaps his attention away from his computer, and his fingers cease flying over the keyboard. "Shut the door."

Oh shit. I'm being fired. I just know it. I do as he says, and with tentative feet, step further into the room.

"Have a seat," he instructs.

On autopilot, feeling like I'm headed to the electric chair, I take a seat in front of his desk. He smiles. It's a really nice smile, he should do it more often. Without a doubt, it's best he fires me, because at the moment I'm about to lose my job, I'm fixated on his lips. The tempting curves and the way the bottom is slightly fuller than the top. I bet he's a great kisser.

"Rose, I've been thinking about yesterday. And I think…" his words trail off.

A boulder sized lump forms in my throat. I've never been fired before today. "If you could not mention on my termination report that I can't orgasm through sex, I'd appreciate it."

"Termination report?"

"Yes. I'm guessing I won't be getting a reference from you?"

He shakes his head. "I'm not firing you."

An audible sigh of relief escapes from me. "You're not?"

"No," he confirms, "I'm going to help you."

"You are?"

He smiles, showing off a perfect set of white teeth. "Yes, Rose."

"Thank you."

"Once we get back from Santa Maria, you can schedule yourself an appointment."

Well, that's not going to work. I can't wait that long. His schedule is packed and my book is so close to being done. "Can't we do a speed therapy? Maybe in Santa Maria we can discuss a few techniques. You can give me a few assignments?"

Something flickers in his eyes before it's quickly snuffed out. He doesn't speak. Oh man, I've rendered a sex therapist speechless. I'm sure this is no small feat.

"Ok, yes," he finally answers. "That's best. We'll get it over fast. I think it will be good for you. I'll put together a little plan."

Oh no, my sex life needs a plan.

"Anything else?"

He shakes his head.

I leave his office feeling like I'm walking a tightrope. One misstep and I'm going to be a broken mess. It's bad enough I have to go on this trip with him, but now I've ensured I'll have to discuss sex with him. If this were in my novel, I'd be saying 'Nah, girl.' But even if I wasn't discussing sex with him, I'd still have to go. One of the best hotels in the Santa Maria area is already booked, a car waiting on us when we arrive—a normal sized one—so it's best to just continue with the plan. The end result will be worth it.

Instead of dwelling on how crazy this is, I make a to do list:

Tell my mother I'll be out of town.

Let the group know I won't be at next week's meeting.

Get non nun like clothes.

~~Research the benefits of avocados for something to talk about with Declan.~~

Find earbuds instead.

Pray for myself.

So much to prepare for.

I text Julie, letting her know my upcoming plans. All of them. And then my phone rings.

"Hello," I whisper into my cell phone.

"You're going on a trip with Sincock and having sex therapy sessions?"

"Shh." I peer over my left shoulder to make sure Declan isn't standing right behind me. "It's business."

"Mhm," she hums, accusingly.

"It is. Nothing will happen."

"I want all the details. And we should probably go over what you're going to pack."

"Pack? Why would we need to go over that?"

"You can't just bring your everyday wear. You need some sexy with it."

I mentally picture my closet. "Yeah, there's no sexy there."

"Well, then we need to go shopping. What are you doing after work?"

My email pings, and I have a new message from Declan, flagged urgent—"We're having dinner tonight to discuss the plan. Pick a place."

So bossy. I answer him with a few taps of the keyboard. "Julie, I have plans tonight."

"What? With who?"

"Dr. Sincock."

"What kind of plans?"

"Dinner and discussing his plan."

"What plan?"

"I don't know. We've said plans so many times, I've forgotten which plan is which."

She laughs. "Ok, call me later."

We hang up and I add one more thing to my to-do list: Do not cross any lines with Dr. Sincock. Immediately, I get rid of that one, 'cause I already have. Instead, I add—do not fall under the Sincock effect.

10

Declan

Many doctors are said to be uptight, not having experience in fun things.

EVERY THOUGHT my brain has had in the past twenty-four hours has been justifying why I'm going to help Rose. Basically, when you cut the bullshit, it's self-serving—I don't want her discussing her sex life with anyone else. Maybe I need my own therapist. No, I need a taco...no not that kind of taco, well, I need that too.

Fuck, what is wrong with me? I'm taking her to dinner now?

While I wait for her outside the restaurant, I scan the court-yard, looking at all the people milling about, wondering if any of them have the same problem as me.

Are they lusting after someone they shouldn't? I mean bosses have dinner with their assistants all the time, right? It isn't against any legal code, or anything. It's perfectly acceptable to have dinner with my secretary. This is not a date, I remind myself, this is business.

"Hi," a quiet voice says behind me.

When I turn around, I'm taken aback for a moment at the

sight of Rose in jeans and a flowy black shirt that exposes the slope of her shoulder. Her long hair is free from the confines she had it in earlier and I have an overwhelming and disturbing urge to sniff it. "Hi. Ready?"

She nods, and we step inside the Burgatory—a local burger joint. To my dismay, the hostess informs us it'll be twenty minutes until we're seated and hands us a little pager thing.

"Want to walk?" I ask Rose, to ease the awkwardness.

She nods, and together we exit and step across the street to a manmade lake. We follow the light-covered path around the water in silence, even though I have so many things I want to talk to her about. Mainly, I want to lay down the foundation of my plan, but figured I should probably feed her first before we get down to the nitty gritty of it all.

"I'm sorry about yesterday," she starts, but I wave off her apology.

"No, there's nothing to be sorry about."

She stops and looks up at me. "I feel like I bombarded you. That maybe I shouldn't have asked for your help."

I slide my hands in my pockets because there's an errant strand of hair that keeps fluttering across her lips, and I want to tuck it behind her ear. "Rose, it's fine. I'm a professional."

So fucking professional I have her here at a restaurant instead of the office because I need a stiff drink to be able to handle discussing sex with her.

"I'm just going to not hold back, ok?"

"What do you mean?"

"Well I don't want you to be…," she trails off, nibbling the corner of her mouth for a moment before continuing, "uptight."

"Uptight?"

"Yes. Sometimes you can be a little uptight and I need you to come down to my level. Get in the dirt with me, so to speak."

"First of all, I am *not* uptight." Why would she even think that about me? I'm fucking fun. "Second, I am not uptight."

She steps closer, searing my bicep with her hand. "I'm on a

deadline, so I need you to talk to me in ways I'll understand, not be stiff. Because I'm stiff. Together, we'd be rigamortis."

The pager vibrates, interrupting my 'what the actual fuck? I am not stiff' moment. Is this how she sees me? I brought her to a burger joint. Nothing says laid back and relaxed like eating beef between a bun with your hands. Well Rose has no idea just how dirty I can get. I'm sediment.

"First lesson, Rose. Feel that vibration in your hand? That's your first step to getting off during sex. Do you have a vibrator?" Wide eyed, she shakes her head no. "Get one. Tease yourself with it." My voice lowers, imagining her legs spread. I lean down to whisper against her ear, "Clit first. Then when your pussy is wet, slip it inside and fuck yourself with it. Find that spot deep inside that makes you grind your hips." A little shiver passes over her body. "Unstiff enough for you?"

"Yes," she says, softly.

Before I step away, I tuck the tempting lock of hair behind her ear. "Ready?"

She nods, and we return to the restaurant at breakneck speed. The only thing stiff about me is my dick. I'm semi hard and need to sit down fast before my cock plows through the restaurant. Rose hands the pager over to the hostess, and we are led to a booth in the back by our server.

Before Rose is even fully seated across from me, she orders a drink. "Can I get a beer? Whichever has the most alcohol."

The dark haired guy laughs at her request and I order a Guinness. When he walks away, Rose opens her menu and I do the same. I've never studied a menu so long in my life. Finally, the server returns with our drinks and takes our order. For me, burger loaded with everything but the chef himself—because I'm adventurous and not stiff—and a bacon cheeseburger for Rose.

When he steps away, she takes a long pull of her beer. "I'll just start," she says, and for the next fifteen minutes, I listen as she explains her jerk ex boyfriends. "So, what do men like? Oral?"

Oh, she goes right for the jugular. I take a chug of my beer. Sure, every guy likes a blow job—it's Heaven on Earth—but sometimes, when you're getting to know a woman, you want to really get to know her before you worry about your own pleasure.

The server slides our plates on the table, and I watch as she takes a bite of her burger. She swallows it all down, then takes a swig from her beer. "I mean, I know guys like that sort of thing."

"Do you?" Oops. it just slipped out. I shouldn't care about what type of lover she is, or if she gives amazing blow jobs, but staring at her lips, it's a no brainer. Those lips would feel amazing wrapped around my cock, or any cock.

She takes another drink from her beer and then stares at me thoughtfully before finally answering, "Well, yeah, I guess I would. I've never actually given one to know if I'd like it."

And now it all becomes so clear, like a crystal shining in the light. Rose isn't just inexperienced—she's *inexperienced*.

"You've never given? Have you ever received?"

"No, ok. Happy?"

I raise a brow. "Happy? No, Rose, it's a shame no one has ever taken care of you." And now I want to be that man. I want to saddle up, trumpets blaring, and ride in on the white horse to rescue the princess from her non-being-taken-care-of tower.

She shrugs. "It's fine. My father was a minister in the local church, so I didn't get out much."

"Yes, *Grace with Gregory*."

Her eyes widen. "Oh, you know who my father is?"

I shrug. "It's not hard to put two and two together."

"Yeah."

"What was it like? Growing up with a father…" I tread carefully, "like that?"

"I went to church every Sunday, and well, I guess you could say I was a good little girl." She laughs a little at her joke.

I try to laugh with her, but hearing her call herself that makes my dick hard. Rock hard. And it's the way she said it—breathy and sweet.

It takes a moment before I can speak again. "So, no guy has ever…." I can't finish my question.

But, she knows what I mean. "No, never."

Now I feel bad she's missed out, and I want to be the one to lick her until she drenches my tongue. But, she's my assistant, so I stick my burger in my mouth before I offer her all the orgasms in the land.

11

Rose

"The most beautiful things are those that madness prompts and reason writes."
—Andre Gide

THE MINUTE I GET HOME, I'm going to go online and order a vibrator. Wish I had one now. Ever since he whispered in my ear, there's been this need low in my belly. I've read about men who are dirty talkers—heck, I'm trying to write one—but no one has ever said those kinds of things to me. And I liked it. A lot. Talking about sex with him wasn't as hard as I thought it would be. He didn't look at me with judgement, or cringe. He actually looked at me the way I envision my hero looking at the heroine when I write. But that must be my three beers and being horny.

We finish off our meal, and on our way out, Declan places his hand on the small of my back, guiding me around a small group at the front of the restaurant. It's intimate and protective, and you'd think he just rescued me from a gang of outlaw bikers by the way I'm acting.

"You can never see the stars much out here," I say, glancing skyward, toward a blanket of stars hidden behind the city lights.

"Yeah, big cities have their consequences. But, I love the city." He puts both hands into the front pockets of his pants, and I almost half-want him to hold my hand as we walk, which means it's time to say goodbye.

"Dinner was nice. Thank you."

"You can't leave yet." His eyes sweep over my face. "I'm going to take you on a little field trip tonight."

"Field trip?"

"Yeah, you'll see."

He leads me away from the pond, toward a wide covered walkway with shops lining either side. It isn't too busy out, and it's a perfect evening for a little stroll. The moon watches from the night sky, lighting the path for us.

I twine my fingers around my black-leather purse strap, glancing in the shop windows. We pass a cute boutique with a bed that looks like a giant bird's nest in the front window.

I stop. "I need this in my life."

He moves beside me. "Seriously?"

I look up at him. "You can't tell me that doesn't look cozy. I'd never want to leave."

He licks his lips, studying me. "You're trying to leave the nest. Why would you want another?"

Hm. "Because peopling is hard. Everyone wants to feel safe and cocooned, don't you think?"

"Maybe you need a turtle shell."

I laugh. "Maybe."

"You have an enchanting laugh, Rose. You should do it more often."

I look away from his intense gaze, because it's making me think things that can't possibly be true. We walk again, and I sneak a peek at his profile.

I wonder what his house looks like? Probably like his office —immaculate with sleek, designer furniture and degrees hanging like artwork on the wall. No bird's nests, I'm sure. Or maybe he's someone else entirely within the confines of his own home. I can't really imagine Declan that way. He's too well-put together. Too structured.

But, I wonder how he lets loose? I mean, he's a sex therapist, so he's not conservative at all.

Now, my parents on the other hand, they never even broached the subject of sex. It was understood that premarital sex was as sinful as it comes. I never even had the birds and the bees talk with my own mother.

But, even though I grew up with strict parents, I do write racy romance novels. So, there ya go.

That's my own little F U to my constraints.

Don't get me wrong, they took good care of me growing up. I was fed, clothed, nice roof over my head. But, the moment I started talking about my dreams of writing, they shut it down. And back then, I hadn't even thought about writing romance. Writing was an outlet to get my feelings down and out of my mind where they'd stay scrambled for too long.

Now, it's fun. And with Declan's help, I hope I can breathe life onto the page instead of being smothered thinking through every sentence. Through every meaning.

I want to live the words I write. And I want to be able to do it for full-time work. Could you imagine? Writing full-time would be a dream come true.

We round a corner, and Declan puts his hand on the small of my back once again, but this time doesn't remove it. I really like his hand on me.

He finally stops in front of a blue door, knocks three times, and a big, burly man with a shaved head answers the door.

"Oh my God, you brought me to a sex club."

Declan whirls around. "What? God, no. This is a VIP club. I wanted you to let your hair down and have fun."

The man at the door allows us entrance after Declan pays the admission cost for both of us.

"This is the field trip?" I look around at the mass of people filling the interior of the club. It's like a secret sin society. All the accents are red: walls, plush couches, even the light sconces hanging on the walls cast a red hue of flames on the dance floor. A dark cherry-wood bar is set in the back of the place, with bartenders wearing red suspenders. This is how he lets loose? Well color me surprised.

"I think you're the type of girl who doesn't go out and have fun very often."

"That's not true," I defend myself. I have lots of fun with Julie. Sure, we don't go to places like this, mainly because I had no idea it existed since it's hidden, but we have fun in our own way. Browsing the bookstore is just as satisfying as this place. "This is what you do for fun?"

"Well, no," he says, moving closer, "but different things can be fun. Even if they seem out of your comfort zone."

"I'm comfortable here," I say, glancing out at the sensual sway of bodies on the dance floor.

Declan crosses his arms. "Really?"

"Yes, really." I want more than anything to show him how wrong he is about me. But, I'm so out of my element here.

He takes a seat on a nearby sofa eyeing me like a hungry wolf. "Dance. Go out there, close your eyes, and just feel the music."

"I can dance," I lie, turning toward the gyrating bodies. Dancing is not my thing. Unless I'm alone. Then I'm Beyonce.

I slip into the crowd and turn to face Declan.

The music is a fast, upbeat song, playing at a deafening level to get people pumped, but I find the hidden rhythm, close my eyes, and slowly sway my hips to the beat. A few bodies brush against me, but I keep my eyes shut, raising my arms above my head and letting the melody slam through me.

I don't dare open my eyes. Declan is probably laughing at how bad of a dancer I am. Not following his directions, I peek open my eyes to see he's not laughing—he's gone.

12

Declan

"What doctors do is a privilege. People let them into the most intimate aspects of their lives, and they look to them to help guide them through very complex and delicate situations."

DAMN, she's hot. I can't turn away from the sexy sway of her hips as she does this seductive slow dance all for me. Or at least I pretend she's dancing just for me.

A few other men watch her shake her ass in her tight jeans, and I stand and cross the dance floor to end up right behind her.

She's sexy and she doesn't even know it, which makes her a hundred percent sexier.

And every man in this club tonight knows it too.

I wrap my arms around her tiny waist, bringing my dick mere inches from bumping into her ass.

I'm crossing a major line with her, this I know, but I can't help myself. And then I take it one step further.

"Imagine a man touching you and getting you off right now," I whisper into her ear.

She turns to face me, her eyes full of innocence. "Will you?"

I breathe out a single 'fuck.' There's no one paying any attention to us on the dance floor now, so, I move her closer to the back, by a wall. I turn her around, and slip my hand along her thigh.

"This is just for educational purposes," I husk out. But I know it's more than that.

She nods and I unzip her zipper, reaching my hand into the top of her jeans.

When I reach the delicate lace of her panties, I groan. Slowly, I run a finger over the fabric and she's already soaked for me.

She moans, leaning her head against my shoulder, exposing the graceful line of her neck. If I were a good man, I'd stop immediately, but I guess I'm not, because there's no stopping what I'm about to do. I lean forward to taste her sweet skin as I move her panties to the side, and take my time getting intimate with her pussy. She's so wet.

"Declan," she breathes out in a whisper.

"Close your eyes." Her hips buck a little when my lips reach the erogenous zone just below her ear.

She's succulent, like a ripe peach, and I keep sucking there while she glides her body in time with my finger, and I enter her, filling her up. Her hand reaches over her head to grab me by the back of my neck. Fingernails dig into my skin, and it urges me on.

I go a little faster now, giving her clit ample attention with my thumb, as I finger fuck her.

She grips me tighter, and I lean into her ear, whispering, "Just let go."

And then someone bumps into us, and she pulls away. "Sorry," the lanky guy says, slurring, before dancing away.

Rose looks like a deer caught in headlights. Her chest moves in short pants, and the realization of just how much I want her levels me like a ton of bricks.

She's as speechless as I am. We stare at each other until she finally finds her voice. "I, uh, have to go." She turns to leave, rushing out of the club.

And I let her go.

13

Rose

"Write while the heat is in you. … The writer who postpones the recording of his thoughts uses an iron which has cooled to burn a hole with."
—Henry David Thoreau

WHAT THE HELL JUST HAPPENED? The night air cools my overheated face as I nearly run toward the lot where I parked. Thank heavens I drove my own car to meet Declan, because the only riding with him I could do right now is astride his cock. Yeah, I said it—cock. It feels like a little chip of naïveté was just removed and even saying cock in my head is easier.

I was so turned on, I should be ashamed. For the record, I'm not. It's scary how much I wanted him. Imagination has nothing on the real thing—the sensations that danced along my skin, the thump of my pulse, the ache between my legs when he whispered in my ear in that husky voice. He's truly a sex god. I wanted to fall at his feet and worship.

The moon now hides behind fat storm clouds, threatening to throw droplets of water on me. I find my car, and head home in a daze, ready to transfer all this emotion to my book. For the first time, I completely let go, imagining he wanted me too. The feeling he gave me in that club is what I've been trying to capture. It was more intense than I ever could've imagined.

The minute I step inside the door, I hustle to my office, fire up my computer, sit down and let my fingers speak for me. They have a lot to say. I write and write.

When exhaustion finally takes over, I push away from my desk and stand, reaching my hands over my head, stretching the aching muscles of my tired back before I cross the hallway to my bedroom, where I remove my clothes, tumble into bed naked, and dream of sultry green eyes.

The next morning, I wake to a knock at my front door. Ugh, it's too early. I kick the covers off and slip on shorts and a T-shirt before answering my front door. A bright eyed Julie, in a light blue T-shirt that matches her hair, stands on my porch. "Morning." She places her hands on her black yoga pant clad hips. "You didn't call."

"I'm sorry. I was writing when I got home." She steps inside and I make my way over to the couch and plop down.

"What happened?" She sits down on the opposite end, pulling a pillow into her lap. "What was the plan?"

"Well, I want you to read something."

"Ok."

I grab my laptop from the coffee table, open the tab I poured my heart and sexiness into, and lean back on the couch as Julie reads the chapter.

Her eyes widen. "Oh, hot damn. Did you write this?"

I nod. "Yes. I was so inspired last night after my first session with Dr. Sincock."

Her head whips over to me. "What? This is based on fact? Spill."

"I still can't believe it really happened."

She sets the laptop on the coffee table. "What happened?"

She listens, dumbfounded, as I tell her how he almost brought me to my first orgasm with a man.

"You just left? No bye, nothing?"

I sigh. "Yeah, I was just overwhelmed. I didn't even say thanks." I'm so selfish. He almost gave me an earth shattering orgasm and I gave him nothing except the view of my back on the way out.

"I don't think you'll need those sessions anyways." She points to my computer screen. "Pru will flip out when she reads these scenes."

"Yeah, maybe she'll hire me to ghostwrite for her."

This makes Julie laugh, but I may be serious.

I worry no one will buy my book, but at the same time, I wonder if I even want people to read it. It's a scary business, one where you put your heart into something only to have people either love it like you do, or tear it to shreds in their reviews. So, you have to constantly debate over every word choice, every action of the characters. But last night was different. I felt it. *Really* felt the words. And honestly, I think my tame sex scenes are cured. We leave tomorrow, and I'm not sure if I can handle being alone with him after last night.

"You and him stuck in a car for about three hours should be fun." Julie fans herself. "I'll pray for you, girl."

I laugh, but I need all the prayers I can get. If I were smart, I'd end this. But now that I know what it feels like to truly desire someone all the way into your bones, I want more.

14

Declan

"Wherever the art of Medicine is loved, there is also a love of Humanity. "
—— Hippocrates

SUNDAY MORNING, bright and early I show up at Rose's apartment, knocking on her front door. I'm not really sure what to say to her when I see her, but before I can really even think about it she flings the door open, "Thanks for the almost orgasm."

My eyebrows shoot up in shock. "You're welcome."

She lets out a sigh. "Sorry, I didn't want you to think I was rude because I just rushed out." She closes her eyes for a moment. "It's awkward now, isn't it?"

I chuckle. "Let's just take it for what it was, ok?"

Her blue eyes peer up at me. "What was it?"

"It was me helping you out."

She nods. "Right. And I have to say, I think I'm cured."

"That so?" She's not cured. No way. I know I'm good, but come on, no one is *that* good. And even if she is cured, maybe I need one more shot with her to make sure she is.

70

"Yeah. It's a miracle."

She disappears inside for a moment to grab her bag and then steps back out to lock the door. My eyes do a quick travel down her body. She's casual again today— dark skinny jeans, red loose fitting blouse, black flats—and looks phenomenal. I should probably make jeans mandatory at work. Or maybe not. Maybe she should wear a tarp.

I take her bag from her and we walk to the car, silent. I'm not even going to touch the subject of how she thinks our sessions are over before they even started. Because not on my watch. Not after last night.

"Ready?" I ask, once we're settled in the car.

She holds up her phone with earbuds attached, and nods. "I am."

And then she pops the buds into her ears and turns to look out the window. Well if I thought we would be talking on the car ride, I guess I'm wrong.

I pull out of her driveway, heading straight out of town. If she doesn't want to talk, fine.

Two can play this game.

I turn up the radio and continue onto the interstate toward Santa Maria.

About an hour into the drive, Rose turns to face me, finally taking the buds out of her ears. "Are you hungry?"

"Very." Hungry for her pussy but food will have to do. I spot an exit coming up with a diner on the sign and nod toward it. "Diner sound good?"

She smiles. "Yes."

Thank god. I need out of this confined space. The entire time we've been driving, I'd love to say I've been thinking about the convention, or my speech I'm supposed to give to my peers in the medical industry, but I haven't. I've been thinking about Rose grinding on my hand. The way she moaned. The way she looked. It's probably the prettiest thing I've ever seen. I've been with my share of women and never felt the animalistic pull I did last night with Rose.

I turn into the parking lot of Mae's Diner, find a space, and shut the engine off. Time to ease the tension.

"Are you going to be quiet the whole trip?" I ask.

"Quite possibly." She opens her door and exits my car.

That went well. Maybe she just needs some time to process. I drum my fingers on the steering wheel while she stretches beside the window. Her shirt rises a bit, exposing a delectable sliver of skin. I've lost my fucking mind. You'd think I've been locked away in a monastery the way I'm acting.

When the semi subsides, I get out and follow her into the diner. We take a seat in a red, vinyl booth near the back. I try again, because she's like an itch that won't go away. "You can't be quiet forever."

Her cheeks flame, and it's adorable. "I guess I'm just embarrassed."

"For what? Almost giving you an…"

"Stop," she cuts me off. "Don't say it."

"It's nothing to be ashamed of." And it isn't. It's a beautiful thing.

My friend, Booker, says, it's the closest you get to Heaven itself. Or in my case, Hell…because that's exactly where I'll be if I keep picturing Rose when I come.

"You're helping me, but you're also my boss." The server drops off two steaming cups of coffee, and once she's gone, Rose leans in. "I'm having a hard time discussing it with you. Maybe we could call it something else?"

She's right; I am her boss. I need to remain professional here. It's hard enough to get respect as a sex therapist in a community where sex is still a taboo topic to discuss, and now I've gone and crossed major lines with my assistant.

I need to get back on course.

I need to fucking focus.

I should fire her. Because having an assistant who drives you crazy is never helpful.

"Like what?" I sip my coffee, black, and stare right at Rose who is avoiding all eye contact by endlessly stirring cream into her cup. "The gift?"

She finally looks up at me, smiling. "Yes, that's perfect."

Fuck me. This girl sets my heart on fire. When I agreed to help her, I didn't really intend on being the one to touch her, but damn if I'm not ready to do it again.

The waitress arrives to take our order and it's nice to know Rose isn't one of those women reluctant to eat in front of a man. She orders French toast, scrambled eggs, bacon, home fries, and a side of fruit. "Got to be healthy," she says with a wink.

It's cute, and the fact I think it's cute is reason to be worried. To get my head back in the game, I change the subject to business, and the next fifteen minutes we discuss the seminar. Rose morphs back into super assistant mode, citing my schedule from memory. Things feel almost normal again until the server slides our plates on the table. By the time we're done eating, I kind of wish Rose *were* one of those women who nibble like a rabbit. It's a sensual experience watching her lips close around the fork tines, watching the way the tip of her tongue peeks out to lick the corner of her mouth. I've never fixated on these things and wished I was a piece of bacon. This really has to stop.

We finish up and get back on the road. Before her ear buds go back in, I get an explanation. "Listening to an audio book."

"Ah, which one."

"The Crux."

"Great book."

She looks a little shocked by my answer. "You read?"

I laugh a little. "Of course, I read. You think I'm no fun and illiterate?"

"Well I didn't mean it like that." She hesitates before continuing, "You're always so focused on work. I imagine you reading medical journals. Just always working. Even at home."

"Is that a bad thing? Work is important."

"If you're passionate about it, it's not a bad thing. Are you?"

"It pays well."

"Ah." I glance over and the way she's studying me makes me feel like she can see right inside my skin to where all the important things are hidden. It's a little unnerving.

"What does 'ah' mean?" I can't help but ask.

"Don't think I didn't notice you didn't say yes."

She pops her earbuds back in and her questions seep into my psyche. I don't hate what I do. Do I get a thrill going in every day? No. But does anyone? Well Jonah seems to. And Chelsea. And Booker and Ethan. Ok, maybe some people do. When I chose to be in an office every day instead of an emergency room, money was the determining factor. Nothing wrong with that. When you're mapping out your life, you usually pick the road that leads to success, not happiness. Right? Honestly, helping Rose is the biggest thrill I've gotten from all my sex knowledge. It's not that I don't care about my patients, it just doesn't give me that high my friends seem to exude about their jobs. Or the high from the clinic. Maybe it's best Rose doesn't talk to me, because now she has me rethinking my life choices.

We spend the rest of the drive in relative silence and finally pull into the Four Seasons. After checking in, we cross the marble lobby and take the elevator to the third floor where our rooms are next to each other.

She stops at her door, gripping her suitcase handle. "We're going to have another session, right? You have a plan?"

I should say no. But I don't. "Yes, see you in an hour for dinner," I tell her, heading into my room. Heading right to the shower to get ready for tonight. And yes, that means jerking the fuck off. No way can I do this tonight and have my dick raring to go.

I turn the water on, letting the steam fill the bathroom, fogging up the mirrors. My clothes are gone in an instant, and I step into the shower. The hot water soothes the tense muscles in my neck and shoulders from traveling with Rose. It feels good, and my cock is already hard just at the thought of making her come.

I'd love to be able to get off at the exact moment she does. Even if things were different, and we didn't work together, it's not an easy task. Most women fake it, after the guy comes, just to end the sex. Cause let's face it, the sex is over for most guys once they come. But, I don't like that idea. Why can't sex keep going?

That's why I like to get the woman I'm with off a few times before I finally orgasm. Some men look at it as a chore. Like 'Ok, to get mine, I have to give the girl hers first, so ugh, let's go.'

Not me. I enjoy making a girl come so hard she can't fucking think straight.

I've talked to many men who say they don't know what a woman wants. They don't know how to make *her* feel good.

And here's where I'm going to let you in on the biggest secret ever. Turning a woman on isn't about where you touch her, or if you're even doing it right. The thing that turns on both male and females is one basic thing: being wanted.

Yes, it's that easy.

A woman wants to feel sexy. She wants to know she's the only woman making your dick hard. She wants to be the only woman who makes you groan the way you are when you touch her for the first time. A woman wants to know that she has your full undivided attention, and that there isn't any other woman on the planet that is making you as hard as she does.

She wants to be the one to make you cry out. She wants to be the one to make you come harder than you ever have. And she wants to be the one whose name you're whispering when you kiss below her ear.

And you know what...it's the same fucking thing for men. We want to make our woman scream our names when she's coming so hard her nails are drawing blood from our skin.

So, when I say these things, this is what I mean: if your girl turns you on so much you can't breathe properly, then you'll want to be the one to put a big ol' smile on her face. Not only will you want to, you'll enjoy all the ways how to.

That's my philosophy.

And I live by it.

I soap my body, working the suds over each muscle and joint. My cock jerks, waiting for me to take it in my hands. I want this orgasm. I need it.

So I grab my dick, wrapping my fingers around tightly, running my thumb over the tip. And then I get to work, thinking of Rose on her knees before me, her red lips slightly parted, her blue eyes gazing up at me like I own the world. I'd conquer all I could for one taste of her sweet ruby lips. I'd wage war on anyone who'd ever try to come in the way of her lips wrapping around the head of my cock.

God, I can picture it. It's so fucking real. I can't even remember the last time I jerked off to such a vivid image.

Water cascades over my head as I continue pumping my dick.

Why can't these images be real? Why can't this really happen between me and her? Fuck, my chest heaves as I picture her sucking me off.

She's got all the makings of being a pro in the bedroom. I bet she gives just as good as she gets.

My cock grows harder and harder as I keep pumping, keep fucking my hand until my orgasm explodes. Fuck me. I place my hand against the tile to catch my breath.

Now it's time to get my game face on and get ready. I dress in black jeans and a black Polo and head down to the hotel restaurant where I spot Rose already seated and ordering a drink.

She's the color of sin in a short red dress. I'm going to keep it simple. Help her, and that's it. Because I know one thing's for certain—as much as I want Rose, I can't have her.

15

Rose

"Plot is people. Human emotions and desires founded on the realities of life, working at cross purposes, getting hotter and fiercer as they strike against each other until finally there's an explosion—that's Plot."
—Leigh Brackett

HE HAS A PLAN. Does he have a plan to kill the butterflies swarming in my belly? Does he have a plan to stop me from blushing every time he stares in my direction?

I should just be happy with my almost climax and call this off. But, more than ever, I want to follow my dream. I saw the look on Declan's face when I asked about his job, and it makes me wonder what he'd rather be doing? So, I'm going to see this through.

But, then again, maybe I don't need it. I mean, Stephen King doesn't need to go around killing people to get ideas for his next novel. Maybe it's all in my head.

Maybe it's time to admit I kind of want Declan to get me off. I mean, I'm sure he's really *really* good at it. Speak of the devil. Like a very sexy bad omen, he approaches my table looking like a dark angel. His light brown hair is carelessly perfect and I want nothing more than to run my fingers through it.

Have you ever heard the expression 'takes my breath away'? Those types of lines are all things I avoid when I'm writing. Sure, it sounds romantic, but how do you stop breathing at the mere sight of someone? Thought it was used by people being over dramatic about spotting a handsome guy from across the room. I get it now, because I can't freaking breathe. He's too good-looking. It just isn't fair to other men. I mean, we live in LA, the land of the beautiful, and I still haven't seen anyone who compares.

"Been waiting long?" he asks, taking a seat.

I shake my head. "Not at all." Twenty minutes isn't long, is it? I'm already under the Sincock effect, because I'm ready to tell him I'd wait a million years.

And I do *not* like waiting. I'll go to every check out aisle in the grocery store, measuring up how many items they have, wasting time just to save time. What's wrong with me? I never act like this toward men. I'd never let a man's looks cloud my judgement toward him.

I have to remember Declan is my boss. The boss who sends me on ridiculous errands and makes me murder muffins before noon on weekdays.

"Red looks good on you," he surprises me by saying.

A warmth settles low in my belly at his compliment. I'll be honest, they say women dress for other women, but tonight, I wore this dress for him. "Thank you. Jeans look good on you."

He smirks and I'm fully expecting an 'I know,' but the server immediately arrives to take his drink order.

Once he's ordered a beer, his eyes stay pinned on me. I'm nervous as hell. My heart is beating so wildly I don't think even a Fitbit could track it. I chew on the bottom of my lip, waiting for his plan.

"Tomorrow we have to be in the convention center by eight," he finally says.

I nod. "Right. Everything is prepared." The minor detail that we are actually here for something besides *me* keeps slipping my mind.

"Tonight, I figured we could do some exercises after dinner?"

Ah, exercises is what he's calling it. Hopefully, he's not referring to the gym in the hotel. "Ok."

"Maybe get to know each other more. I know I've already, well…"

He can't even say the words, and I can't even think them. "Yes, the gift."

"But, if this is going to work, we need to familiarize ourselves. I need to know what turns you on."

This is going to be harder than I thought, because I don't even know what turns me on. He pulls a pair of black frames from his pocket to read the menu and I realize, glasses turn me on. It really turns me on.

"What?" he asks over the top of his menu.

"Nothing." I tear my eyes from him to my menu, staring at the picture of fresh lump crab cakes instead of him.

He laughs, setting down his menu. "Come on, do I look like an idiot?" He points to the sexy black-rimmed glasses perched atop his nose.

"No," I answer, honestly. "Quite the opposite, really."

The server arrives to take our order and gives me a wink and a 'My favorite. I knew I liked you.' when I go with the crab cakes. He's a cute guy—brown hair, baby blues, and a smile that probably gets him really good tips—but he doesn't make my panties wet. That's my new standard. So far, only the man across from me meets it.

Declan orders the same, and as soon as the server leaves the table, professes, "I don't like him."

I let out a small laugh. "Why? Because he didn't say he liked you too?"

"Yeah, like he was eye-fucking you over a crab cake."

"Maybe it's because you didn't get the slaw like I did."

He rakes his teeth over his bottom lip. "Listen, I know what men are thinking."

"No you don't. Not all men."

"Yes, all men."

I glance around the restaurant and spot a balding man in a black suit, sitting next to a brunette probably half his age. I give a head nod over to them. "What's he thinking?"

Declan turns in his chair to get a better look. "He's wondering how much more money he's going to have to shell out to get her to touch his dick."

My eyes widen. "No, he isn't."

"Oh, yes he is."

I spy another server by the entrance to the kitchen, staring our way. "And him?"

"Ah," Declan leans in, and then so do I, "he's checking you out because our server told him there was a bombshell of a redhead at this table."

I can't help but smile. "I don't think you're right."

Declan leans back, removing his napkin from the table and setting it in his lap. "I know I'm right. It wasn't the slaw."

I like the way I feel when I'm around Declan. More confident and sexy. It's something I'm not used to, and I could get high off this feeling.

The more I'm around him in a non-work setting the more I like being around him in a non-work setting. Crazy, I know.

I don't want to ruin this moment with my own selfish agenda so I keep it light and ask the question I've been dying to know. "What's it like being related to a movie star?" His sister is *the* Chelsea Sincock.

He laughs a little. "She hasn't always been famous, but yeah, in the beginning it was a lot of craziness. The paparazzi would follow me around hoping to get a scoop on her." He takes a drink of beer. "But then it settled down. She's married to my best friend, Jonah."

"That must have been tough for you, having your best friend and sister dating."

He gives me a wry smile. "Well, they got married before they dated." Reading my mind, he waves his hand, shooing away the questions I have. "It's a long story. Yes, at first it was hard to deal with, but they're perfect for each other."

"She's a talented actress."

"Yeah," he agrees. "My other best friend is Ethan Hale."

"Ethan Hale?" I have a slight fan girl moment. "Can you bring him to the company Christmas party?"

"Hey, now." He laughs. "You wouldn't like him."

"He's great in the movies."

Declan shakes his head, teasing me. "He's awful."

I laugh. "You're lying."

"Yeah, he is pretty great," he admits. There is an indiscernible gleam in his eye when he stares at me from across the table. "He'd like you."

Our dinner arrives, and we chat about Hollywood for a bit, and Declan tells me the story of how Chelsea and Ethan became famous. He loves his sister and friends, that fact resonates in what he tells me. It's a very attractive quality.

After our dinner is cleared, Declan pays the check, denying my attempt to pay for mine, and we stand to leave.

And now I'm back to being nervous as he leads me out of the restaurant, once again with his hand on the small of my back.

"Let me walk you to your room," he says.

"For exercise?" I kind of blurt out. "I hope you mean our session, because if I have to get on a treadmill, I might lose my crab cakes."

He stops walking just outside the lobby, near the elevator. "Yes, Rose, for our session."

Phew. I'm seventy-five percent excited and twenty-five percent anxious, or vice versa. I one hundred percent can't wait to have Declan's hands all over me.

He presses the elevator button and says in a low voice, "And I won't be touching you tonight."

I blink. "Why?" Now listen, obviously this is the best plan, but I'm a little let down.

Then it dawns on me, maybe he doesn't *want* to touch me again.

"I just mean, we shouldn't do anything that crosses any major lines."

We step into the elevator and I select our floor from the panel. "Lines, right."

"I'm just saying we shouldn't go there, because sometimes feelings get involved."

"Ah." My face heats with a little anger at his comment. "I'll be sure no feelings get mixed into this. Sure thing, Doc."

He steps closer, frustration emanating from his tall body. "I didn't mean it that way. I'm trying to be professional, but it's really fucking hard."

He looks a little tortured saying that to me, and I wonder if it's my fault because he's feeling like I can't be professional about this too. "It's fine," I assure him. "I agree with you."

He lets out a deep breath. "Good."

Yes sirree, I can be as professional as they get.

16

Declan

A doctor named Duncan MacDougall once tried to prove the existence of the human soul.

IS WATCHING Rose get herself off considered professional? That's what I want to do. I want to watch her brace her small feet on the bed and dip her fingers inside herself.

And no, I've never done this with any other patients. Rose is a first for me. She's kind of a first for a lot of things, actually. Like one, I've never had these types of convos with my assistants before. Two, I've never had a strong sexual pull toward any of my assistants before. And three, I just like being around her. And that's a new one for me.

Don't get me wrong, I enjoy the company of the opposite sex plenty. But, never just to hang out and chill. And I could see myself chilling with Rose all night. And never once even touch her. Like tonight.

My plan is to not touch her—that's the plan—and by God I will stick to it. I have to. I can't call myself a professional, if I don't.

I'll keep my hands to myself, no matter how hard it gets. Pun intended.

And I'm sure it will get very hard. Hell, I've been fighting a semi all night. Jerking off in the shower did nothing to stave off this crazy sexual tension. And now, I have to fight another urge to not grab this redhead of a temptress and kiss the hell out of her. I really want to kiss her, suck her tongue into my mouth, nip that plump lower lip with my teeth. If we don't get off this elevator soon, I might do it.

I survive the ride and walk down the hallway with her, leaving ample space between us. She slides in her keycard, and the loud click of the lock being released reminds me I'm entering forbidden territory. She opens her hotel room door, and knowing I shouldn't, I follow her in. It all feels so tense, like I should make a joke or something to cut some of this tension in the air.

"Nice room," is all I can come up with. All humor and joke-worthy jokes leave my brain when I look at the bed and see a black bra in the midst of the white comforter.

"Thanks, my overbearing boss had me book it." She smiles. "I guess he has good taste."

"That he does." The rooms are large, but we might as well be in a cardboard box. I step away, taking a seat in one of the navy wingback chairs positioned by a small desk on the other side of the room. "Have a seat, Rose." No sense wasting time.

"Oh ok." She perches on the mini sofa. "This all feels very professional. Don't you think?"

"Very." Except for the dirty thoughts running through my head.

"So, what is the exercise?"

"I want to show you how to ask for what you want."

Her face now matches the color of her hair. "Ok," she says, softly.

"Unless you're not comfortable with that. I would never make you do anything you're not comfortable with."

"No, no, it's not that. I feel safe with you." She sighs. "It's hard for me to let go. Even in my mind…" she fiddles with the hem of her dress, hesitating, "…It's a subconscious thing. I want to be dirty—I feel like I can be dirty—but it's hard to let it out. The other night with you is the first time…well, that I let go."

Her words cause a sensation of alpha male pride to wash through me. I make my girl feel safe. Well, pretending if she were mine. But she's not. I blow out a deep breath. And let's not even touch on the dirty girl part or my cock might burst through my pants.

I clear my throat. "What would you want a man to do?"

"What do you mean?" she asks so damn innocently.

"To get you aroused."

"Oh." She blushes. "I'll tell you one of my fantasies?"

Hearing her say the word fantasy has my dick perking up just a bit to see what's going on. "Sure."

"Well," she leans back, "I want a man kissing down my neck." She lightly trails her fingers down the column of her throat, and I can picture myself planting those soft kisses along her sweet skin.

"Keep going," I husk out.

"Well, we're in an elevator. I picture his hands roaming all over me and then he wants me so bad he picks me up and we slam back against the wall."

Fuck, this is better than porn. I should stop asking her questions and just leave the room.

I try to think about Gross Anatomy in med school. I try to think about my Great Aunt Meredith. I try to think about anything but her hands running up and down her sweet little body.

Too late now. I'm in this, and I'll see this through.

I shake my head, hoping to disperse the lust haze fogging my mind. "Close your eyes, Rose." She obeys. "What are you thinking about?"

"Your hands on me."

Oh fuck again. I try to push aside the fact she said 'your' and try to remember she's probably in a state of arousal imagining her fantasy and sometimes words spoken at this heightened sense are sometimes misconstrued. Or basically she doesn't mean them. But, fuck it. "Where do you want me to touch you?"

Lines crossed. I hear the siren loud in my mind, reminding me to back away, stop the whatever it is I'm doing with her and slow down.

I suck in a deep breath, my body unable to cool down on demand. When I let it out slowly, she knocks my world off its axis.

"I want your fingers deep inside my pussy."

Her neck is on display for me, looking silky and grabbable. I just want to wrap my long fingers around the column of her throat, kiss her deeply, and thrust my cock straight up inside her.

But first, I want to hear her say that word again. "What else do you want me to do?"

Maybe I should move onto the couch?

No, I need to sit my ass in this chair, and not move. I wish I could strap myself in. Then, I wouldn't be tempted.

"Touch my breasts, play with my nipples."

I stand. I have to.

I have a job to do here, and I'll make sure I'm the best at it. She needs to know what she wants. She needs to be confident. All women should.

I want to lean over—well let's face it, I want to do a whole lot of fucking things to her. I've already felt her slick pussy and how tight she is—but, I know if I touch her again, I'll never be able to stop.

So I slide my hands in my pockets, wanting more than anything to release my dick from my pants and slam it into her. "And then what?"

"I don't know."

"You want my mouth on you?"

Her eyes fly open. "Yes."

"What about my cock, Rose? Do you want my cock inside you?"

"Yes."

Her breasts strain against the silky material of her dress as her chest rises and falls. I think I'm breathing just as fast as she is. I hate helping her so some other jack off can come along and touch her. On fire, I walk toward her, lean in nearly nose to nose and brace my hands against the back of the couch. She sucks in a quick intake of air.

"See how easy it is to say those things? Don't be afraid to tell your man how and where to touch you. Because it's sexy as fuck hearing you say it. And by God, have the confidence to tell him what you like. If you never tell him what you like, then you're leading him right into failure by not giving him a roadmap to all the things that get you off. And if he can't give you what you need, he's a fucking fool. If you were mine, I'd fuck you the right way til you come so hard, you'd feel me in your soul." She swallows, hard, and I take a few steps back. Fuck me. "See you in the morning."

I stalk to the door and leave. Next lesson she's on her own. There's no way I can do that again and keep my hands to myself.

17

Rose

"To gain your own voice, you have to forget about having it heard."
    —Allen Ginsberg

THE WORD of the day is professional. You'd never know by looking at us—me in a black pencil skirt, white blouse, hair secured tightly at the base of my neck and Declan in black Armani with a tie that matches his eyes—that I actually said I wanted his fingers in my pussy. I said that, and I meant it. None of these men and women gathered to hear Declan speak about the philosophy of sexual health know I said I wanted him to play with my nipples. But, I am the epitome of professionalism. I have zero feelings about any of it.

"Do you have my notes?" Declan asks in the small waiting area off stage at the convention center.

"They're in your inbox." Since I am professional, I emailed them last night after I was left near orgasm. I'm ok with it. And I'm definitely not feeling insecure about the fact when we met up this morning there was no mention of last night. I'm professional; I got this shit.

He opens his laptop, pulls up his PowerPoint presentation, and then tabs over to check his email. "Ah here it is," he says. "Two minutes to showtime."

"Good luck. You got this."

"Thanks, I always get nervous speaking in front of large crowds." He looks out at the podium and rubs the back of his neck.

He always seem so in control. And then I think about all the times he normally has me cancel these types of events. Or how he declines awards that would cause him to speak in front of a crowd. It never crossed my mind Declan hated public speaking. I'm realizing I've made assumptions about someone I really knew nothing about. My eyes meet his. "You know the material backwards and forwards." I lean closer. "Just picture everyone naked."

The announcer calls his name and the room fills with applause. Declan glances out on stage and then back at me. "I'd rather picture you naked."

My eyes widen, and then he walks away to take his spot behind the podium. His sensual voice resonates throughout the space without wavering. He probably doesn't look nervous at all to the people listening. But I see the miniscule crack in his armor. It's in the tightness of his smile and his hands gripping the podium. There's a shyness about him. A sexy, confident shyness if there ever were such a thing.

It's easy to put myself in his shoes. My father lives for these moments, relishes the attention, but that gene skipped right over me.

He speaks to the crowd, but I'm not paying attention to the words. Instead, I watch every little tick of his jaw, every pull of his muscles underneath his white Oxford. He's truly spectacular. The crowd is captivated by what he tells them, and I find myself captivated for a different reason. Not because I'm interested in the philosophy of sexual health, but because I'm interested in the man saying the words.

I've never seen Declan as human—flesh and blood with feelings. I've always seen him as my overbearing boss. The boss who sends me on ridiculous errands, and barks orders at me. But he's also the boss who let me have the whole week off when my mother was sick. The boss who asks me everyday how I'm doing.

The same boss that agreed to help me, no questions asked. That same exact boss who touched me in a way no other man has ever touched me.

I'm so awful, and *so* letting feelings get involved. I'm not professional at all.

At the end of his presentation, he thanks the crowd and then makes his way toward me backstage. And now, I'm the one who's nervous.

"Let's get out of here," he says, loosening his tie.

"Don't you want to hear the rest of the seminar?"

"No, I don't."

We pack up his things, and exit into the hallway.

"Where are we going?" I ask as we walk briskly down the long corridor.

"To change and then we're going to the Pier."

"Really?" I'm a lot excited because I didn't think there would be any sight seeing this trip.

We hustle back to the hotel and I quickly change into jeans, white T-shirt, and Chucks. When I exit my room, Declan lounges against the wall in well-worn jeans, short-sleeved, navy Polo that hugs his biceps, and an LA Dodgers ball cap. The ball cap is definitely equivalent to the glasses on the 'turns me on' scale. He's like a chameleon transforming into different shades of sexy.

Twenty minutes later, we arrive at the double jointed pier, and enter under a colorful wooden sign. I breathe in the smell of popcorn and laughter in the air. It's a little wonderland placed right on the Pacific Ocean, and as Declan purchases tickets I stand back, watching the waves crash to the shore.

"I love it here," I tell Declan as we enter the midland toward the games on either side.

"What do you want to do first? Hungry?"

"Starved."

He smiles and leads me over to where a vendor sells funnel cakes. He buys one and we share the sweet treat doused in heaven as we walk around looking at all the rides. "I'll ride anything you want except the roller coaster," he says before sucking powdered sugar off the tip of his index finger.

"Why not the rollercoaster?"

He stops walking, finishing off his last bite of the funnel cake before chucking the paper plate in the trash. "No reason. Just not a fun ride."

I peer upward at the bright colored track. "Really? I've never been on it. Looks fun, though."

"Trust me, it's not."

I look over at him. "It's not because you're afraid of heights, is it?"

"Of course not," he denies, but I don't believe him.

"I'll be with you."

He raises a brow in my direction. "I love heights. In fact, I'm not afraid of anything."

"Except public speaking."

He raises a finger to tsk me. "I never said I was scared, just that it made me nervous."

"Like the same kind of nervous the rollercoaster makes you?"

He winks. "Careful, Miss Thorne. I might have to write you up for insubordination."

For some reason, I find his playful remark hot. I really wish he'd stop making me like him by showing me this side of him. This is getting way out of control.

We walk around, riding a few rides, playing a few games, ignoring the obvious tension between us until it's time to go.

Before we leave, Declan wins a stuffed baby goat with devil horns shooting hoops and hands it over to me.

"Are you sure?" I ask as we walk toward the pier entrance.

"Yeah, don't girls like that stuff?"

I smile. "This girl does."

He wets his lips and gives me a lazy smile that makes my heart do this weird flip in my chest. "Good."

If this were in my book, this is when he'd kiss her. He'd stop walking, lean in, splay his hands against her cheeks, and crash his lips to hers. But this isn't a romance novel and I make an awkward joke instead. "Might have to hide it if my Dad comes over."

"Your father never let you have any experiences, huh?"

"Sure he did." I smile when our eyes meet. "As long as it was of the church variety."

"I have nothing against church," Declan says. "I just believe sex, relationships, and things like that are something that should be between the couple, not God."

I fondle the horns on the baby goat and speak the truth, "I agree."

"Any brothers or sisters?" he asks.

I shake my head. "Nope, only child. You? Well, I know you have Chelsea, anyone else?"

"Nope, just Chels and me."

Instead of heading to the exit, he veers toward the roller-coaster. "We don't have to," I tell him.

"No way am I not going to ride it with you."

"It's really ok," I assure him.

"No."

We step into the line, and I grab a hold of his hand to reassure him. "It'll be ok."

Some things just go together—chips and salsa, apple pie and ice cream, Han Solo and Chewbacca—and that's how my hand feels in his. Like it belongs with it. He looks down at our joined hands but doesn't pull away.

"It's not safe," he says into my ear.

I glance up. "It's been here a long time. I'm sure it's ok."

"Exactly. It's old and decrepit."

We move forward at a rapid pace and are seated near the back. He places his hat under his leg, and when we're buckled in, I make the sign of the cross over my chest, even though I'm not Catholic, and look over at him. "When I said I hadn't been on this, I meant I've never been on a rollercoaster before."

His head snaps to me. "What? This is your first time?"

We inch forward. "Yeah."

"So your everything will be ok was a lie?"

"Yeah, pretty much."

"You're a child of God, you're not supposed to lie."

I'm probably not supposed to let my boss finger me either, so hopefully I'll get a pass. "Sometimes we have to do what's best, not what's right." We move forward a little faster, and to the right, waves crash against the shore. "That view, though."

"Yeah, it's stunning."

We pick up speed, dipping and turning, and I don't know if the adrenaline in my veins is from the high of the ride or the fact his eyes never left my face when he said the view was stunning.

THAT ROLLERCOASTER YESTERDAY is definitely a metaphor for my life. I feel like I'm free falling—of my own free will—into something I won't recover from. When Declan and I arrived back to our hotel, it was late. If it had been a date, he would've kissed me. But it wasn't a date, and there was no kiss. We said goodnight, and after stepping inside my room, I couldn't sleep. So I opened my laptop and wrote. I couldn't do anything but write about longing so sharp you don't feel the slice until you're bleeding. And then I got to the blow job scene. Cue the record scratch. I've never done the act per se, but after being around Declan all day, that's right where the story lead me.

Annette and the man she wants are at a high-society ball. Elaborate masks hide their identities, and Annette has to find him out of all the men at the party. Obviously I made that hard for her, because she can't just go traipsing up to him. No, Annette's got to work for her man. After torturing her a bit, building the tension, she found him. She knows his hands. They're skillful hands. Protective hands. She's a minx, so she leads him into a small restroom and drops to her knees to give him one of the best blowjobs he's ever had.

Except, Annette picked the wrong hands. She's about to blow the wrong man with the right hands.

Her enemy. I love my story so far. There's depth to the characters; it's not all sex. I'm sure Pru wouldn't think so, but the sex scenes I've added since working with Declan are on fire. We have one more day and then it's back to before, so I need to make what's left of our time count.

Today was spent in lectures and being professional—no lazy smiles and seductive winks— and tonight, right now, we're at a goodbye dinner party. I'm going to get a little more help, hopefully of the blowjob variety, and then I'm on my own.

Declan pulls me a bit closer on the dance floor and like our hands, our bodies just go together. This event is like living in a fairytale. It's all so posh and upscale. I've never been to a party this extravagant before, well unless you count the endless church functions my mother would host, but those don't count because I never had any fun at them.

When I made the decision to remain professional with Declan, it was difficult at first. Seeing him in his tuxedo, hair gelled just perfectly, and his green eyes pinned on me, it was really hard to keep him at an arm's length.

It got easier as the night progressed. Until he cut in on my dance with James Clifford.

Which don't get me wrong, I'm so glad he did. James is a

perv and a half. He kept asking me what I was doing after the party, and if he could drive me home—three hours away. Yeah, no thank you, I watch *Law & Order*. I know he's respected in the medical community, but still, I'm happy for the reprieve, even if that reprieve is Declan.

He tugs me closer, his hand resting just above the curve of my ass, and I breathe in his forbidden scent. Everything about him is perfect tonight, and I'm half-ready to beg him to claim me. But, I won't do it. Even though tiny demons are screaming at me from inside my head to rip his tuxedo off and beg him for an orgasm. When did I become this needy?

"You look beautiful tonight," he whispers close to my ear, breaking me from my naughty thoughts. My black lace cocktail dress is demure yet not, stopping above my knee and sheer above my breasts leaving hints of skin. The real sex appeal is on my feet, slinky black heels with a thin strap around my ankle.

"Thank you," I whisper back.

He does a lopsided grin that if I were wearing panties, would make them wet.

Tonight, I want to be daring like Annette in my novel. She wouldn't wait to give this man the best blow job around, no she'd march over to him and pull him into a corner and do it right then and there.

Here goes nothing.

I smile up at Declan with my best seductress stare.

"What?" he asks. But, I ignore him, getting into the mindset of Annette. "What are you doing?" he asks a little more dumbfounded this time.

"Follow me." I grab his hand and lead him off the dance floor.

I can't believe I'm really doing this. I'm going to blow him.

18

Declan

Life sometimes speaks in doctorisms...

"DR. SINCOCK," a tall dark haired man calls out to me as I'm being led through the ballroom by Rose. "Ignore him," she whispers. That's pretty easy to do with the way she's dressed. She is undeniably the sexiest little thing here in a black dress that worships her body. And fuck, she looks fantastic. I can tell others agree, by the way men's eyes gaze at her as if she's got all their research answers hidden beneath her dress. Jealousy snakes its way through my limbs, until I remember this is not a date. She's my assistant. Which is really laughable. A lot of other doctors here have their assistants and office staff by their sides, but they aren't looking at them like I'm looking at Rose.

"Dr. Sincock," the gruff voice says again. This time, he stalks over, impeding Rose's progress. She stops, dropping my hand, and then I realize it's Houston Dale, a prestigious surgeon from New York.

"Dr. Dale," we shake hands, "how are you?"

"Good." His dark eyes flit to Rose. "Houston Dale," he introduces himself, shaking her hand.

"Rose Thorne. I'll just leave you two alone," she says, excusing herself, obviously unaware she's in the presence of greatness. Not me, Dr. Dale. Well, I'm great too, but that's not in question. Before I can stop her, she's weaving through the people scattered about the ballroom.

"I just wanted to let you know your speech was impressive," Houston tells me, dragging my attention back to him. "My wife is a psychiatrist, and has read some of your papers."

"Thank you. Is she here?"

"No, couldn't make it." He gives a head nod toward the direction Rose went. "Is that your girlfriend?"

"My assistant."

His brow rises. "Ah. Been there, done that. She's my wife now." I feel like I'm suffocating. "I probably had that look on my face too. Your larynx is probably closing, making you feel like you can't breathe. That's the worst fucking feeling, man. You'll survive."

I rub a hand down my face. "Yeah, it's not like that."

"It is," he says, matter of fact. "My wife would say you're suppressing your emotions. The bigger they are, the harder they fall."

"No falling is taking place," I assure him.

"You can tell me that again at your wedding." He smiles. "I actually wanted to talk to you about a business proposition."

"What kind of business proposition?"

"I'm opening my own practice in New York. I've heard great things about you and would be interested in talking further about bringing you on board."

It takes a minute to absorb what he's offering me. "As a sex therapist?"

"No. A medical doctor. I've read your bio, I know you volunteer at a clinic." His dark eyes narrow a bit with contemplation, as if he has some wisdom to impart. "I once taught, and it was ok, but I didn't live and breathe it. Nothing comes close to practicing medicine." He chuckles. "Except, my wife."

I smile. Working with someone like Houston Dale would be a fucking dream. "I'd like to hear more."

"Good," he clasps me on the shoulder, "I'll give you a call and we can talk further."

"Sounds good."

"Have a good night."

He walks away and I force my feet toward the exit. I need to find Rose, and end this.

"Dr. Siiincock, so glad you are here," a female voice coos, drawing my attention.

I spin around and look into the ice blue eyes of Deidre Flanigan, a former colleague of mine. Dark hair piled loosely on top her head shines under the lights as she closes the distance. Her breasts reach me before she does. Deidre has been trying to get on my dick for years, and at one point, I may have entertained the idea. But, I never let myself go there, because we worked together. Apparently that was back when I had ethics.

"Deidre, how are you?"

She places a hand on my arm. "I'm doing much better now that you're here."

My pulse beats an unsteady rhythm. I'm getting agitated and I pull at the bowtie of my tuxedo.

"Well, I'm not going to be much company tonight." I peer back over my shoulder, looking for Rose one more time.

Her blue gown clad body sidles even closer. "Need some stress relief?" I look down at her. Maybe I do. Maybe I do need to fuck Rose out of my system with someone else. "My lips aren't just for talking."

She eyes my dick. Let's face it, I'm screwed in the head. I know most guys in my situation would love having a girl sucking his dick with no expectations for more.

But, maybe I want more.

Maybe, just maybe, I want more with Rose.

God, I need to pull it together.

You think it's easy? It isn't. It isn't easy having strong feelings for your assistant, client. I don't even know what to call her. She's a client slash my assistant, and she's completely off-limits.

I want to check on her. Make sure she's ok, but I know if I knock on her door I won't be able to not touch her.

"The answer is still no," I tell Deirdre. The only lips I want wrapped around my cock are nowhere to be found.

I leave the party and head up to my own room, tearing my suit off the minute I step through the door.

The minibar is my best friend for the next few minutes as I sit in my boxer-briefs chugging little bottles of whiskey until I can't take the silence anymore. I grab my phone, scanning through the contacts for Rose's name.

I text her: *Are you ok?*

She answers back quickly: *Yes. I'm sorry for leaving so soon.*

I reply: *That was Houston Dale. The Dr. Dale.*

And then we keep going…

Rose: He seemed very stern.

Me: He offered me a job in New York. Medical doctor.

Rose: Really? Are you considering it?

Me: Maybe. I don't know.

God, I want more than anything to hear her voice, but instead I lie back against the plethora of pillows on the King-sized bed in my room.

Rose: Why did you become a sex therapist?

Me: Money.

I hold my breath, hoping I haven't scared her off with how callous that sounds.

Rose: Did that money make you happy? You should probably think about that.

I do think about that for a minute. Sure, I get temporary enjoyment out of expensive gadgets, but there's no denying there's a vast hole that can't be filled with things. But I'm solid—

successful—and I have a big ass house... that I go home alone to every night. What more could I want?

Me: Maybe you should have been the therapist.

Rose: Ha! I'll send you my bill.

Me: Where were you taking me?

She doesn't answer for a while. But, then my phone dings.

Rose: I thought I'd get in one last help session, but changed my mind.

I don't text her back, for fear of asking her if I can come over to her room. No matter how much she turns me on, I won't have sex with her. That's not part of the deal. Tomorrow things go back to normal, and that's for the best. I spend the rest of the night, tossing and turning, wondering what Rose would do if I accepted the position in New York. She'd work for whoever they replaced me with, but would she like them? Would she miss me? As hard as it is to admit, I'd probably miss her annoying ways, amongst other things I don't want to admit to myself. It's the alcohol making me a pussy.

The next morning, we check out and it's like we've morphed back into pre-trip. Rose is back to withdrawn—but still sexy as fuck in white capri pants and a clingy black, v-neck T-shirt—and I'm still studying her like I'm a buyer at a fashion show.

"Here let me grab your bags," I offer, setting my suitcase in the trunk.

"Thank you." Faint dark smudges under her eyes tell me she slept as shitty as I did.

I toss her suitcase in and when I'm pulling away from the hotel, I gaze at her for a second. And rip the band aid off.

"We should talk about what all this means." She remains quiet, so I continue. "The sessions are done, but if you feel you need more, I can refer you to someone."

"No, I'm good." She smiles, slipping on her sunglasses to shield her eyes from me. "Everything is professional."

Narrowing my eyes a bit, I drum my fingers on the steering wheel. "No weird... feelings?"

'Cause I sure have them.

"None. Thank you for your help, Dr. Sincock."

Oh it's like that, huh? I turn up the radio and focus on the road. Things are definitely back to 'normal.' She's a thorn in my fucking side.

———

BEING BACK from Santa Maria feels like the first page of a whole new story. I don't know what happened to me there, but everything feels so different now. Like, I don't know how to act around Rose, even though she made it crystal clear she's harboring no residual thoughts of our sessions.

And I have no time to figure it out because I leave to meet with Houston in New York tomorrow.

This week, since we've been back, she's been her usual distant organized self. And part of me wonders if she's put her new found awareness of what turns her on to use with someone else. As if I summoned her with my thoughts, Rose saunters into my office. "Did you need anything else before I go grab lunch?"

"No, thanks." What I need is for her to not wear a skirt so tight I'd have to peel it away with my tongue. Before I can request she go home and change, she disappears.

For a few minutes I can't get out of my own head. My thoughts roll over and over about Rose and her wardrobe.

In frustration, I push away from my desk just as a blonde walks into my office. "Please tell me you're not my next patient."

"As if." She walks closer, smiling. "I'm sure you'd love to hear all about my sex life though."

"Fucking disgusting." I stand and grab my little sister, Chelsea, in for a big bear hug.

"What's got you all flustered?" she asks when I pull out of the hug.

"What?" I wipe a hand through my hair. "Oh, nothing."

"It isn't the redhead who just left here is it?"

"What redhead?"

My sister swats her pink-tipped nails against my jacket. "I see someone has a crush."

"Stop."

"I've known you my whole life. I've never seen you this worked up over someone before." She narrows her eyes a bit. "Who is she?"

"No one. My assistant."

Chelsea folds her arms. "Is she no one, or your assistant?"

"Neither. Both," I grumble.

"Come on. You can tell me about it over lunch."

I follow Chelsea out the door, leading her across the walkway toward my favorite yellow taco truck.

My eyes scan the afternoon crowd, searching for Rose. She always has lunch alone in the courtyard on the bench under the giant oak tree. But, not today. Now I know why she rushed out of my office.

She's got a lunch date. With a man.

He's around her age, maybe a year or two older, but not her type at all. I can tell. First, he's wearing skinny jeans with purple shoes. And second, he's staring at his phone instead of paying attention to her. She needs someone, well, more like me. But not.

Chelsea steps up to the window to order, and I try to get a better glimpse of the man with Rose.

With our tacos in hand, Chelsea follows my gaze. "Is that your assistant?"

"Yeah, I don't know." I take the taco from her hand and bite into it, thankful for something to keep me from answering her questioning stare.

"You don't know if that's your assistant?" Her arched eyebrow gets higher.

"Yeah, I guess." I try to sound nonchalant, but Chelsea is Chelsea and isn't buying it.

"Let's go say hi."

I stand my ground, firm, not budging an inch. "She's on a date."

"So. I just want to meet the woman who has my brother all tied up in knots." She walks toward them, and I wish more than anything I wasn't following her.

19

Rose

"I can shake off everything as I write; my sorrows disappear, my courage is reborn."
— *Anne Frank*

THIS PHASE of my life should be known as AD-After Declan. Ever since the sessions with Declan, I feel like I'm this whole new person. Like a butterfly that's emerged from its sex repressed chrysalis into a new world. My writing has come to life, thanks to him. Before, it was one dimensional, going through the motions of what I thought someone would feel. Empty words with no real meaning. Now it's nuanced, living and breathing. He's made me more daring with myself, which in turn, is making me more daring with my writing, and my characters. It's a crazy world I'm living in, filled with bright colors and loud noises, and I'm trying my best to keep the two worlds separate.

Since we've been back, I've been trying to cross back over the line where it's safe and familiar. But it's like trying to get over a barbed wire fence naked. He's leaving tomorrow to meet with

Houston Dale and I don't know if I'm glad for the reprieve or sad that he might be going away permanently.

If I'm being honest, it wasn't easy pretending I had no feelings to talk about in his car. Since he'd already warned me not to get confused about his help, I didn't want him to think I couldn't do my job once we got back, so I compartmentalized all those feelings I'm not supposed to have into a little box inside my head and worked it out on the page. I finally wrote 'The End' on my novel. When Christian offered to meet me on my lunch hour today to take a look at it, I was thrilled, because today is the day I'm going to publish. Maybe.

I sit impatiently, on the bench in the courtyard at work, waiting as Christian reads over the ending on my phone.

"So, what do you think?" I ask, a little too needy for approval.

He hands back the phone. "Rose, you've got something special there. I think you're ready. What are you so worried about?"

"No one can know I wrote this."

I may have emerged from my chrysalis but I'm just learning to fly with these baby wings and not quite ready to spring this on my parents. Or Declan.

"Listen," he says, "part of joining the group is signing an NDA not to reveal identities and such. So you don't have to worry about us." He pushes his black-rimmed glasses further up his nose and squints a bit. "Is that who I think it is?"

I peer over my shoulder and spot Chelsea Sincock, in all her superstar glory, walking our way with Declan trailing behind.

"It is." I stand in a rush, shutting my phone off and sliding it into my black satchel. "Her brother is my boss."

He's no longer listening to me, and I can't really blame him; she's even prettier in person.

"You're Chelsea Sincock," Christian says, beaming at her. "I've seen all your movies."

Chelsea smiles back. "Aw. Thank you." She holds out her hand to Christian. "Well, you know me. Who are you?"

"I'm Christian Dennings. Rose's friend."

Declan is a statue, holding a taco, minus avocado, I'm sure, completely mute. His stare penetrates right through my skin, like he wants to touch me with his mind. And subliminally, I'm over here spreading my legs for him to do so.

Chelsea turns to me. "Rose? I've heard so many great things about you."

"Same." We shake hands. "It's so amazing to meet you."

"How do you know Rose?" Declan asks, skewering Christian with his gaze.

I stiffen. "Does anyone really know anyone?" I joke.

"She just showed up on my doorstep one day," Christian deflects with a smile.

Declan's harsh stare scrutinizes us, and now I wish this little meet and greet was over. As cool as it is to meet Chelsea—squee—I want to crawl under a rock and hide until Christian leaves. He asks Chelsea a few questions about her latest movie project and she's gracious and down to earth, filling him in on a few details about her role until Declan interrupts, telling her they should leave Christian and me to whatever we were doing before they arrived.

"It was nice to meet you both," she says before they leave.

Christian continues his pep talk as I peek glances at Declan and Chelsea walking toward the building. They stop, and she gives him a hug before heading towards the parking lot. He glances in our direction, before disappearing into the building.

Christian and I discuss publishing for a few more minutes, and emboldened by his assurances and Harry Potter quotes about breaking the rules and thinking anything is possible if you have the nerve, I say a quick goodbye and hustle back to work.

As is the norm, Declan is sequestered in his office when I return. I open my document and all the things I'll need. I have twenty minutes left of my lunch hour, twenty minutes to give birth. I probably shouldn't be doing this here in the office, but it's sort of ceremonial in a passive aggressive way. It's really only fitting I do it where *Love Doctor* was conceived.

Now, I just have to figure out this publishing garble on my screen and heave this baby out into the world.

I select my genre (Erotica) and type in search words—boss, asshole, scxy, romance, love, hate, professional—until I've reached my allowed limit. A ping sounds from our inter office messaging system and I read the message from Declan flagged urgent.

"If your 'friend' is gone, I'd like a cherry biscuit."

"Didn't you just eat?" I reply back, slightly confused at his single quotations around friend.

"It's dessert."

"Just finishing up something."

I tab back over to Better Books and continue the process.

A ping sounds, and I tab back over.

"Have you left yet?" his message reads, once again marked urgent.

"Yes," I type back.

"Obviously not, since you replied."

Nerves take a rollercoaster loop through my belly when I peek over my shoulder at the closed door. There's no way Dr. Sincock will ever find out he was the muse for my novel.

I tab over to Better Books, and a shiver of excitement racks my shoulders as I move the cursor over and select the file. I'm finally doing it. The blue bar inches across as *Love Doctor* uploads, and I send a little prayer up to whoever is listening that people will be kind to my book baby, and then I finally do it. I hit publish. My celebration is cut short when another ping sounds.

"Can you stop daydreaming about your 'friend' and fill my request?"

This is too much stress. I'm trying to publish a book and pretend I'm not harboring feelings for the man who inspired said secret book. I push away from my desk and stalk into his office. We all have a moment where we crack, this is mine.

"Did you get me that blueberry muffin?" he asks, with a serious expression.

I place my hands on my hips. "It was a cherry biscuit, and no."

A burning starts low in my belly and fans out through each limb as his eyes roam over me, starting at my feet, moving up and then back down.

"I see. So no biscuit is what you're trying to tell me?"

I nod.

He stands and strides across the room. "You know what this means, don't you?" I shake my head. "It means I'll just have to eat you instead."

And then, he kisses me.

A full-force kiss. It's like gale force lust knocked my sails over, and I'm no longer churning through the fierce ocean, but floating into him.

I open my mouth to him, and his hand glides along my collarbone to slip behind my neck. I don't think it could get any better until he deepens the kiss, twirling his tongue with mine. I moan, and he swallows it down in a hungry attempt to get closer.

"Why do you have to be so sexy?" I ask as he pulls away to nibble the base of my neck.

"I know the feeling," he says back.

And then, our lips lock once again and I'm no longer the lone ship on the ocean, no, I'm the little bird flying high and spreading my wings for the very first time.

His greedy hands roam my body as if he's never touched anyone else before in his life.

And I'm glad he's taking control right now, because I can no longer even remember my own name.

20

Declan

"To solve a difficult problem in medicine, don't study it directly, but rather pursue a curiosity about nature and the rest will follow. Do basic research. "

I WALK BACKWARDS WITH HER, leaning against my desk, and then I sit on it, bringing her with me to straddle my lap.

"You're absolutely wrong for me," I tell her, kissing her lips once more.

"There's never been anyone more wrong for me."

I keep kissing her, keep sucking and tugging her tongue into my mouth, and at the same time, grinding her hips into me.

"You're so infuriating. Do you know that?" My anger mashes together with the extreme lust swimming through my body.

"I hate how right you always think you are," she murmurs. "And who doesn't like avocados?"

I stop kissing her neck. "Everybody."

Her eyes lock with mine, hungry, eager, so damn beautiful, and my heart bangs around in my rib cage. My erection is painful, to the point I might just take her now, forget about being right or wrong.

"You kiss me like you've never wanted anyone this much," she whispers.

"Christ," I murmur, "I never have."

She pulls back just a bit, and her innocent eyes greet mine. "You haven't?"

I shake my head, barely able to breathe as her hips grind against me. "No."

"You want me?"

I fight every urge to kiss her, lay her down, move in and out of her, show her just how bad I want her. Instead, I grab her hand, rubbing it over the hardness straining against my zipper. "This is how bad I want you, Rose."

Her pink tongue darts out to wet her plump lips. "I can't believe you're so…"

"Hard?" I finish for her.

Her cheeks flush. "Big."

Jesus. I kiss her. I kiss her because all I can do *is* kiss her. It's the only way I can control the situation. I want her to get off. I want to make her orgasm. But I need to keep my body in check.

"Tell me, Rose. Tell me you've never wanted anyone this bad."

"Yes to everything."

"The thought of how wet you might be is driving me insane." Blood pounds in my ears. "Are you wet for me?"

"Very." She moves in to kiss me again, but I hold her by the hair, not letting our mouths touch just yet. She tries to grind against me but I hold her still with the other hand on her hip. She lets out a whimper, and it's probably the sexiest sound I've ever heard.

"I'm going to make you come, Rose. I want you to drench your panties with it. I want you to move against me like your life depends on it. Got it?"

Her eyes search mine, questioning. "So, is this a follow-up appointment?"

God. I want to scream no. I want to tell her this is *so* much more for me. Instead, I kiss along her throat, the side of her neck, and nibble on the lobe of her ear until she is once again moving against me.

"I want those panties to be soaked just for me. Make them so wet for me."

I keep using my hands to rock her hips into me, so she can come. She rides me, dry-humping me with her eyes closed, her head tilted forward, her lips-bruised and plump—begging to be kissed more.

I need to keep my heart out of it. I need to keep my head in the game, even though every cell in my body vibrates with lust.

Her tits press up against me, her chest heaving, and I reach a hand up to cup one. It fits perfectly in my hand, so much so that I can't stop kneading it with my palm.

"I'm so close," she whispers against the shell of my ear.

I return my hand to her ass, helping her get off.

"Come all over those panties for me," I say, dragging my teeth against her collarbone.

She grips the back of my shoulders, runs her fingers into my hair briefly, and then back to my shoulders, gripping my shirt in her hands. "I'm coming," she moans in a throaty whisper.

"Fuck, Rose."

She rocks and rocks, her body lifting slightly, bringing her tits even with my mouth. I reach out, nibbling the stiff peak through her shirt.

She rides out her orgasm and I could never be prepared for how beautiful it is. Bliss filled blue eyes stare back at me. And I can't stop looking at her. I simply can't turn away.

The moment she comes down from her glorious high, she drops her forehead to mine. I run my fingers through her hair, smoothing down the edges.

"I'm going to need those panties, Rose," I whisper against her lips.

She stands and slides the scrap of material down her legs, stepping one heel out of them and then the other. Pink. She hands them over and her breath catches when I rub them against my cock before slipping them in my pants pocket.

My phone rings interrupting our moment and it's like the sound brings us back to the reality of where we are.

"I'll let you get that," she says, transforming into business Rose. "I have some things to print out before your next patient."

Right, I actually have a job to do. The phone continues ringing, demanding to be answered. I rise and adjust myself before answering. "Dr. Sincock."

"It's Houston Dale."

"Hello, Dr. Dale." Rose breaks her stare from mine and exits, closing the door.

With Rose's panties burning a hole in my pocket, I spend the next fifteen minutes hearing what Houston has to offer. It's a lot. He wants me to fly out tomorrow night, meet him in person, and scope out the area. I agree.

When I hang up, I find Rose seated at her desk. "I'm flying out to New York tomorrow." What horrible fucking timing.

"For the job?"

"Yeah," I answer, raking a hand through my hair.

"Oh, that's great." Great? She doesn't want a replay of what just happened? 'Cause I sure do. "I'll get your flight scheduled and your hotel. How long will you be gone?"

"It's ok, I can book it." This all feels wrong. I don't know how to separate work from the fact I just made her come.

"Why? Is it because..." she hesitates, "...I'm still your employee, Declan. We need to be professional, even if you have my panties."

Hearing her call me by my first name is like a punch in the chest. Maybe it's best I'm going away for a few days. She's right, we have to be professional. To drive that fact home, my next patient arrives. While Mrs. Winston updates her paperwork, I return to my office and email Rose the trip information.

The rest of the afternoon is spent with back to back patients that run over time. By the time, my last patient leaves, Rose is gone for the day. When I check my email, an itinerary is sent to me from Rose with a note that reads, "Have a good trip. I'll talk to you when you get back."

I grab hold of the panties in my pocket, knowing full well she won't be getting these back anytime soon.

They're mine.

———

THE NEXT MORNING, I dribble the ball and make a three-pointer as Jonah groans behind me.

"Nice shot," Jonah says.

"I'm feeling extra lucky today." And I do. I have like a pep in my step or something. I wipe the sweat from my brow.

The park where we shoot hoops is filled with families, sitting on blankets, basking in the sun, or couples walking hand-in-hand with sniffing dogs trailing behind as Jonah and I shoot hoops on one of the parks four basketball courts. We have the one closest to the road, and I've been using that to my advantage by acting like there's something important going on over Jonah's shoulder so when he has the ball he might take a quick peek. But, he's onto me, and my usual playful tactics haven't been working out so well for me the past few minutes.

"...you've got to ask yourself one question: Do I feel lucky? Well, do ya, punk?" Jonah rattles off a line from *Dirty Harry* and I smile.

"I actually am feeling pretty good."

Jonah shoots the ball and scores on me. "What's up? Why so jolly?"

I laugh at his word choice. "I met this doctor at the convention, Dr. Houston Dale, anyway he offered me a job."

Jonah stops dribbling for a second, all serious now, holding the ball with one hand, and says, "That's great news. What did you say?"

"Well, I don't really know yet."

Jonah goes back to dribbling the ball before handing it off to me. "What's not to know?"

I stand out of bounds, check, then begin dribbling. "It's in New York. I'm flying out tonight to spend a few days to meet with him."

Jonah stands straight, no longer trying to get the ball from me. "No shit?"

I nod and cross the court to the makeshift bench closest to the other courts, set the ball down, and grab my water bottle to take a sip.

Jonah follows behind me, blowing out a deep breath. "Well, that ...sucks ass. I mean, I'm happy for you and all, and I only say it sucks for selfish reasons."

"I don't know if I'm going to take it."

Jonah grabs his own water bottle. "Why wouldn't you take it?"

My mind flits to Rose, to kissing her in my office, to making her come, and I lift my shirt to wipe a few beads of sweat off my brow. "I don't know. It's definitely something I don't want to make a rash decision about. This is my home." My family is here. How can I just pick up and move halfway across the country? How does one even make that choice?

And now after kissing Rose, it's all kinds of complicated.

I take a seat on the bench.

Jonah sits beside me. "Sometimes choices in life aren't easy, and sometimes you have to make them for everything else to fall into place."

"What movie is that from?" I ask with a smirk.

Jonah shakes his head. "No movie. It's a Jonah Marshall original."

"Thanks, man."

"I think you should take it."

I nod. "Dr. Dale is kind of my hero. Have you read his articles on the medical therapies of acute myocardial infarction by application of hemodynamic subsets?"

Jonah raises a brow. "Now why would I have ever read that?"

I laugh a little. "Ok, let's just say the guy's a genius. And he mentioned his wife is a therapist so he's excited to bring me on."

"I'm really proud of you." Jonah slaps me on the shoulder. "You deserve this. All that time in medical school shouldn't be wasted."

I know he's right. And I try to picture my life there. Busy streets, a paper coffee cup in my hand—because it just seems everyone in New York holds a latte in their hand—subway terminals, a city that never sleeps.

It wouldn't be much different from Los Angeles. But, still, something nags at me, something not letting me jump for joy over the offer.

And that something is Rose.

21

Declan

"In nothing do men more nearly approach the gods than in giving health to men."
—*Marcus Tullius Cicero*

NEW YORK IS Metropolis by day and Gotham at night. Skyscrapers draped in fog and good and evil sharing space on the crowded sidewalks. I want to beam a big D into the sky for Rose. Pretty sure she needs the D.

I try to picture myself living here, taking the subway to and from work everyday. The vibe is a hectic one, traffic clogging the arteries of the city, everyone rushing around. The pulse of the city that never sleeps is alive with vibrant noises, chaos, and madness.

I can picture it all.

And just for one split second, I can see her with me. Rose.

Her walking the streets with me, stopping for coffee at the local shop. Maybe heading into the park for an afternoon of laziness together.

Would she even want to do those things?

When I arrive at Houston's office where we're meeting, a dark haired woman, behind a reception desk, smiles at me. "I'm here to meet with Dr. Dale," I say to her. "Declan Sincock."

She types on her computer. "Just have a seat and I'll tell him you're here, Dr. Sincock." She smiles once more, pointing to an area with mini gray sofas and leather chairs in the lobby.

I tap the counter and thank her, but before I can even make it a few steps, Dr. Dale is stepping off the elevator with his phone pressed to his ear.

He spots me and disconnects the call.

He smiles as he steps off the lift, his hand outstretched to shake mine. "Dr. Sincock, how was your flight?"

"It was all fine." I study the spacious marble floored lobby with its pops of colorful flowers and high tech visual stimulation. Everything perfectly planned to make waiting less excruciating, right down to a few massage chairs and a charging station for professionals. "This is quite some place you have here, Dr. Dale."

"Houston, please call me, Houston."

"Ok, Houston. Nice place you have here."

He laughs, slapping his hand on the back of my shoulder. "Let me show you around."

For the next hour he does just that, taking me up to the top floor first where his office sits right next to his wife's, with my office (if I take the job) right down the hallway.

"Marley, this is Dr. Sincock." Houston leads me into his wife's office, and the brown haired woman sitting behind the desk glances up.

"Declan Sincock, I've heard so much about you." She stands, and I shake her hand. "It's nice to meet you."

We talk shop for an hour or so before Houston invites me to dinner and drinks in the lounge of my hotel. We relax in brown leather chairs, sipping bourbon, and looking like every other gentlemen in here. It's a bit pretentious, but I'm enjoying myself all the same.

"So, what do you think of the practice?" Houston asks, leaning back, one arm outstretched over the back of the leather.

I grab my bourbon on the rocks and swirl the liquor around in the glass. "It's all...perfect."

Houston is perceptive and raises a brow. "But, it's not for you?"

I shake my head. "No, it isn't that at all. I'd be honored to work here, it's just..." How do I explain Rose?

How do I explain I don't...can't leave her?

"It's just the assistant?" Houston brings his drink to his lips and takes a sip with a knowing smile.

I don't like her being referred to as 'just the assistant.' "There's nothing 'just' about her," I correct him. "Her name is *Rose* and if it weren't for her, my life would be chaos."

"Good answer." He smirks. "That's exactly the type of response I would give about my Marley. She's now the mother of my beautiful daughter—Angela."

I raise my glass to him. "Congratulations."

"Angela is definitely a little *diva*." Houston sets his glass down, steepling his fingers together. "Life sneaks up on you in more ways than one."

Ain't that the truth. I shouldn't even be considering Rose in this decision, but for some reason she's all I can think about. I want to say yes, because with every fiber of my being I want to have this job. I want to live in New York.

"It does," I answer, bringing my drink to my lips and swallowing it down.

This is a dream come true, it really is. "So, what do you say?" Houston asks.

———

IT'S LATE by the time I get back to my hotel room. The off-white walls with their gray stripes make me feel caged. Bourbon swims through my veins, making me a little more brave when I grab my phone, pressing Rose's name. It's earlier in California, and I send her a text, *"How's your night going?"*

A few minutes later she answers back, *"Life is grand. How's New York?"*

I imagine her with the setting sun as her backdrop, her red hair blowing in the California breeze, and it makes my dick hard. *"It's missing one thing."*

"Oh, what's that?"

"You."

She doesn't answer for a while, so I press her name on my phone and hit the phone icon. It rings twice before she answers, "Hello."

"Hey," I say to her. "Did I scare you off?"

"No. I kind of wish I was with you tonight too." I can hear the stress in her voice.

"Is everything ok?" I ask, moving over to lie on the bed.

"Yeah, just a rough day. Enough about me. How was the job? Are you going to take it?"

Who cares about my day. "Why was it rough?"

She giggles into the phone for a second. "No, it's much better now. Are you taking the job?"

I blow out a deep breath. "I am." I want her to talk me out of it. I want her to tell me she doesn't want me to move clear across the country away from her. I want her to tell me no.

But, she does the opposite. "I'm so happy for you."

And there it is. Cut and dry. Black and white. Plain and simple.

But, it's not good enough for me. And it's not good enough while I fly back to Cali, her words slicing through my brain over and over. It's still not enough when I catch a cab from the airport and give the driver her address.

Because *this* is not good enough.

22

Rose

"A professional writer is an amateur who didn't quit."
    —Richard Bach

I *AM* A PUBLISHED AUTHOR. I say it again a few more times, letting the sound of it roll off the tip of my tongue. It feels good. And it feels even better that I've sold a few books. Very few. I can't believe I sold one book let alone a few.

I've been on an endless loop refreshing my sales since I published. I'd check them now, but there's no time. My last group meeting is tonight. I've done some thinking and somewhere since joining the critique group, I've lost the sense of writing for myself. I feel like I'm writing more for the approval of Pru and the others in the group. And somewhere along the way, I lost the whole sense as to why I wanted to become a writer in the first place.

When I emailed everyone to let them know this would be my last meeting, Christian and Rebecca were sad, but understanding. Pru couldn't care less.

I dart around my house, throwing on grey cotton shorts and

a pink Dodgers T-shirt, getting ready for my last meeting. After putting my hair in a low ponytail, I grab my purse, dig around for gloss, and apply some in the mirror hanging in the entryway. My reflection looks the same, but I feel different. I have *so* many feelings. Ever heard of kismet? It's like, for example, you spill your coffee, but the man you were meant to fall in love with helps you clean it up. Not that I'm in love, mind you. I was looking for explanations of what's going on with myself and Declan, because I'm that type of person, and I don't think I could've avoided what's happened between us. Pru criticizing my sex scenes and setting off this chain of events, was just all part of destiny. Or maybe I'm making excuses for my choices.

Either way, I don't know where Declan and I go from here. Back to normal? I hope not, 'cause actually, I want more. Is that too naive of me to want more? If you set the bar low, you can't be disappointed. My bar is sitting on the ground.

He's going to New York to work with Houston Dale and obviously he's attracted to me, but I don't have a magic vagina to keep him here. And even if I did, I couldn't do that when I know he wants the job. So many unanswered questions.

I don't have time to dwell on the answers, because there's a knock at my door. I check the peephole to see Pru, in a loud psychedelic dress with black Mary Jane's, peeping back at me. Rebecca and Christian stand behind her, and I open the door and welcome them in.

Pru's eyes sweep around my apartment assessing everything —the dark hardwoods, buttery walls, tall windows with floral drapes, red sectional—like she's a prospective tenant. "I had you pegged for something more... beige."

Of course she would. Ignoring her remark, I lead them toward the living room where we do our normal thing for the next hour. At the end of the meeting, when they're getting ready to leave, I tell them my news about *Love Doctor*.

Rebecca's green eyes light up. "That's awesome. I'll look for it."

"Thank you so much."

"Congratulations, Rose," Christian beams.

"What's the book about?" Pru asks, pulling her keys from her bag.

"It's an office romance." Her brows go up with interest. "Annette meets a man she's interested in, but when she's supposed to find him at a masquerade ball, she ends up finding her boss instead, unknowingly."

"How's it selling?" Pru's insinuation rings loud and clear.

I cross my arms, to avoid giving her the finger. "Well it's only been a few days," I answer.

"Mm, so it's not selling," she guesses correctly.

"I think it's going to do great," Christian says, coming to my defense.

"Thank you."

"You know," Rebecca looks over at Pru, "not everyone has your tricks. Some people actually write their books and get where they are because of talent and hard work. I'm sure you and your team will be working behind the scenes casting doubt about the competition."

She gives me a hug. "Congratulations again."

"It's ok," I say, softly, "I'm just happy I finally did it."

After they're gone, it's like a weight has been lifted. It's freeing not being chained to Pru's negativity any longer. That freedom doesn't last long, because before I can walk ten steps, there's a knock on my door. Hopefully it's either Christian or Rebecca who forgot something and not the Wicked Witch. I open it, and it's none of the three. It's Declan.

He looks… like he wants to rip my clothes off with his teeth.

"Hi," I breathe.

"You're...gorgeous…" he husks out, barely above a whisper.

And then his arm is around me, bringing me closer as his lips descend on mine. I cling to him as he devours my mouth, walking me back into my house and shutting the door. Our tongues meet, and a moan escapes me.

"Rose," he whispers against my lips.

My eyes barely flit open.

"I need you. And this isn't any ordinary need. The only things we actually need are things to survive—air, water, and food. But, added to my list is your sweet pussy, because I will die if I don't get it right now, and there's no exaggeration about that."

My heart stops.

His hands run down my sides, ending at my ass.

With our lips still connected, he picks me up as my legs instinctively fly around his waist.

"Bedroom?" he asks.

"Last room. Down the hall," I direct him, pointing to the back of my apartment.

I feel like I'm in a novel. I didn't think something like this really existed. But it does. I could kiss this man forever. My mind has a million thoughts spinning around inside, each one trying to surface, but I can't think straight. I can't breathe in my own head. I haven't seen him since I handed over my panties, so I wasn't sure how to act, or what to expect when he returned, and in all the scenarios I came up with, it never included this.

My skin hums, my heart beats frantically, and my body yearns—freaking yearns for this man.

No part of me is left untouched. He moves his hands all over me, caressing everywhere that aches for him.

My fingers explore his hard chest, ending at the hem of his t-shirt and bringing it over his head. He helps me take it the rest of the way off, and all I can do is ogle his chest.

Muscles everywhere, hard and magnificent. I lick my lips, wanting more than anything to run my tongue right down the middle of his abs. And then I do. His skin is silk over steel.

"Damn, Rose." His breathing comes out in short pants and then he lifts my babydoll tee over my body, stripping me down to my white, lace bra.

His hooded green eyes make me feel drunk, and I like the way he stares, unabashed, unafraid to show me he desires me.

And I have never in my life felt as sexy as I do right now with his eyes on me. I can't think about anything in this moment. Not the job in New York or my book. All I *can* think about is him.

He bends his head down, landing his perfect mouth on the skin just above my breast and then removing my bra to suck my nipple in between his teeth. Ah, it feels so good.

I drag my fingers through his hair, pulling and gripping, bringing his lips back up to meet mine.

Our bodies move in tandem, both of us wanting more from the other, knowing full well this won't end until he's buried deep inside me.

He kisses my neck, up to my earlobe, nipping it with his teeth. "Rose, tell me you need me, please," he begs in a husky whisper.

"I need you." And I do, more than anything. Because I may not ever get another chance with him ever again.

He hoists me up and we land on the bed. The remainder of our clothes disappear in a blur of eager hands. He spreads my legs, running his finger through my wetness, and then fists his jutting dick, pumping it from base to tip. It's just so big.

"I'm not sure it'll fit."

He smiles. "It'll fit, Baby. I can promise you that." And then he wraps his dick with a condom, positioning the head of it right at my entrance, pushing slowly into me. Inch by thick inch. "Ah fuck," he groans as his eyes never stray from mine. "You feel so good. So wet and tight," he murmurs as he pushes deeper.

The last of the sun's rays make their way across the wall of my bedroom, skittering the room in a soft glow, and I cling onto Declan a little tighter, afraid to let go of him. I want to make sure this is all real. That it's not a dream, even though every single minute of it feels like a fantasy.

He pushes deeper, and ah, it's so hard, so very big, and so unmistakably real.

And when I think it couldn't feel any better, he moves his chiseled hips, and thrusts. "God, Rose, fuck…" he whispers.

Lost in the exquisite torture, I dig my nails into his back and he groans loudly, kissing the column of my throat, and nipping his teeth along my collarbone.

This is no ordinary fuck, this is fate.

Our bodies slide together and he lifts my hips, going deeper.

I want to live in the moment with him right now, relishing the sensations he's causing through my body. I want to take everything he's giving and give it back. Make it count. I want to be dirty. I slide my leg onto his shoulder and reach down to fondle his balls.

His moan is my reward. "Rose, fuck."

I love the way he says my name. The way he breathes it. Owns it.

He rolls his hips, reaching a spot deep within me I didn't know existed. All I know is I am now ruined. When he leaves, I will spend the rest of my life trying to recreate this magic and failing.

"You feel me there, Rose?" God the look on his face. "I'm marking what's mine."

"Declan," I murmur, unable to hold on much longer, "don't stop."

"I can't stop."

And I don't want him to. I don't want him to leave. Just like that I'm falling for this man. So hard I'm going to shatter.

He braces his arm on the bed and I turn my head to lick the quivering muscle in his forearm. His dick stretches me and I feel it coming, starting low in my belly, building with each stroke until an intense orgasm rushes through me, exploding through every cell in my body, running to the ends of my toes, curling through my fingers.

His eyes capture mine, and the emotion coursing through me makes me bite my lower lip to keep control of myself.

He runs his hand through my hair. "Rose, I got you." And then he kisses my lips, his tongue dancing along mine in a tango of sweet desire. "I got you, Baby."

And he does, his body holding mine in place, as he pumps inside me. I raise my hands, cupping his cheeks, staring into his eyes. "Don't let go."

He shakes his head, closing his eyes as he thrusts a few more times. He groans my name out, as his body tenses, shuddering with his orgasm.

We try to catch our breath. Declan's still inside me, and I almost don't want to break this magical spell. I know once it's all over, we go back to boss/employee. Therapist/client. Friend/friend.

And I don't think I want that anymore.

He kisses my forehead and moves off me before heading into the adjoining bathroom to clean up. When he returns, neither of us say a word as he crawls into bed behind me, pulling the covers around us like a cocoon. He wraps me into him, spooning our bodies together.

"I like this," he says.

"Me too."

How do I ask him to stay? Do I even want him to?

I do.

More than anything.

His fingers trace along my back, and an uneasiness settles over me, wondering if he's waiting for just the right moment to dash out the door and never look back.

"If you have somewhere you need to go…" my words trail off when he turns me to face him.

His green eyes blaze right through me. "I'm not going anywhere." Then the sheepish grin appears. "If that's ok with you."

"Do you normally stay?"

"Depends."

"On?"

He props up on an elbow, tucking a stray strand of my hair behind my ear with the other hand. "I'm not going to lie to you, Rose. I usually don't stay long."

"Why not?"

He doesn't answer right away, his eyes drifting around the room like he doesn't quite know how to word what he's trying to tell me. "Let's just say I've never cared enough to stick around."

"There's nothing wrong with that." Sure it's the tired old story, playboy runs around on women, having one-night stand after one-night stand, but at least he's being honest. "Declan," I start, unsure of how to word exactly what I want to say.

"What is it?" He continues to strum his fingers through my hair.

"You always told me to tell any man I'm with what I want."

"What do you want?"

You. I want to scream, but instead, because I know he's leaving soon, I try to hold onto him a bit longer. "I want to spend as much time with you as possible before you leave." He doesn't say anything. "Like a no-strings kind of thing," I quickly add.

He leans into where his lips are a mere millimeter away from mine. "I can do that for you."

And just like that the sense of his job in New York looms off in the distance, but I close my eyes trying to pretend to myself that it isn't real. That he won't really leave.

He kisses me, and his hands travel through my hair. And then, we're touching and grabbing each other all over again, and this time I know I won't have to say goodbye any time soon.

23

Declan

Becoming a doctor takes a great amount of schooling, and in that time many things will be learned and experienced, but you can still never predict the final outcome.

RIGHT BEFORE I fall asleep with Rose tucked safely into the crook of my arm, I think about her words, 'no-strings' and shake my head.

Oh, there'll be strings all right, if I have anything to say about it.

The next morning, I yawn and stretch, rolling over in bed to find the spot next to me empty. "Rose?" I sit up, rubbing away the sleep from my eyes.

"I don't want you to leave," she says, standing in her robe by the bedroom door.

She smiles that radiant smile of hers, and I know she's talking about today and not New York. "I don't want to." And I'm being fucking honest here. I hold my arms out, swatting the side of the bed next to me.

She bounds on the bed, wrapping her arms around me, and

I curl her into my chest. "Hungry?"

She gazes up at me as soon as I release my hold on her. "What did you have in mind?"

"Get dressed." I smack her playfully on the ass. "You'll see."

After I run out to grab my bags I brought straight from the airport, I dress in jeans and a black tee.

Rose steps out of her bathroom. "I'm ready."

"You look amazing."

She looks down at her denim shorts, white t-shirt with a giant pair of lips on it, and pink sneakers. "Thanks," she smiles, giving me a little pose, "this is my Target wear."

"I'll send them a thank you letter."

She laughs, swatting me away. "Where are we going?"

"One of my favorite places."

She grabs her keys and tosses them to me. "You can drive, if that's ok with you."

"Sure."

Outside the sun peeks over the San Gabriel mountains, lighting Rose's hair to a brilliant shade of fiery red. It looks good on her, and it's something I won't soon forget. Just like I won't forget the no strings thing. With a fresh coat of paint to start the day, there are so many possibilities, so many ways to charm her into adding maybe one or two strings to the deal.

We hop in her Camry, and I take off down the street. In the car, I grab her hand, kissing along her sweet skin.

She opens her mouth as if she wants to say something important. You can see the exact moment in her eyes when she must decide against it, and says, "You could give me a hint."

"I could, but where's the fun in that?"

She yanks her hand away from me. "You're so mean."

I grab her hand back, bringing it to my lips once again. "You sure like being in control, do you know that?"

She glances over at me, her baby blues glistening in the soft sunlight. "I do not."

"Oh yes, you do." I laugh a little. "I think it's sexy."

She pulls my hand to her lips, and kisses along my knuckles. "Two can play at this game." She lets go of my hand, running her fingers up the inside of her thigh. "Want to see more?"

I try to pay attention to driving, but it's getting harder and harder to keep my eyes on the road. "What are you doing?"

"Nothing," she says, her fingers running over the edge of her shorts to the spot in between her thighs.

"Doesn't look that way." But, before she can get any further I pull into the vast parking lot, filling up for this afternoon's Major League game. "I can drive around the block a few times if you want to keep going." And that is complete honesty.

She smiles and opens her door. "Nope. Let's go."

I shut the car off and step out of the driver's side door. The smell of hot dogs and popcorn fill the air as we draw closer to the front of the stadium. I fucking love baseball. It's America's favorite pastime, right?

"I used to come here a lot when I was a kid, and even still now." I walk her to the ticket booth. "Two please," I say to the man behind the glass.

Her eyes light up as she glances around the ballpark to take it all in. It's fun watching her. "I think I like it." She smiles up at me. "I've never been here before. Are they any good?" she asks, pointing to a picture of the LA Dodgers baseball team.

My eyes go wide. "Shh, people will hear you." I grab her hand after I've paid for the tickets. "Of course, they're good. One of the best teams in the league."

"Ah, well I can't wait to see."

"That's my girl." And I pull her closer to me, wrapping my arm around her shoulders.

I don't know what it is about her, but I have a thing for touching her. Like my greedy hands are magnetically drawn to every part of her.

We enter the stadium and head for our light blue seats.

"Do you like all sports? Or just baseball?" she asks as we sit down.

I glance around, looking for someone selling hot dogs. "All. Golf is my favorite."

"Ah," she says, smiling. "Well, you seem like a golf guy."

"A golf guy? What exactly is that?"

"Someone who plays golf."

I laugh. "Are you saying because I'm a doctor, related to a movie star, and live in a nice house that I'm a golf guy?"

"No," she denies. "It just seems like a rich man's sport, maybe."

"I'll have you know I wasn't always rich."

"We're opposites." Her eyes connect with mine. "I grew up very rich and now don't have a lot."

"How does that work?"

She shrugs, and I spot the hotdog guy out of the corner of my eye and raise my hand to call him over. "My mother and father don't believe in the same things I do."

"God?"

"No. Just life choices and such."

I meet her eyes. "They don't like your job?"

She laughs. "They don't view it the same."

"Why not?" I grab my wallet. "Hungry?"

She nods and then answers, "Because you're a sex therapist. And sex is not something to talk about out loud. I've actually never told my parents what type of therapist you are."

"Ah ok." I order two dogs and two soft drinks. "You just avoid it?"

She stares out at the field. "Yeah."

"They should be proud of you. You're excellent at your job." And I'm telling the truth.

She looks over and winks. "I am very detailed."

"You shouldn't hide who you are. Some people will surprise you."

The game starts and after a while Rose really gets into it. She cheers from the stands and smiles more than I've ever seen her smile. And I'm having fun. More fun than I can remember having in a long time.

"I can see why you like coming here," she says, right before she gets nailed with a foul ball.

24

Rose

"I don't need an alarm clock. My ideas wake me."
—Ray Bradbury

THERE ARE NO PEARLY GATES. There's a ticket booth with a glass encased window and a towering man selling hot dogs. Honestly, I don't care for hot dogs, and I have no money to get into heaven, because my book isn't selling.

"Can I charge it?" I ask the man at the booth. He's very handsome with just a hint of scruff.

"Charge what?"

"Heaven." It's very sterile here. "I'm sure you wouldn't let me in anyway, I've been very judgy about my boss. I like him a lot."

He shines a bright light in my eyes, causing me to squint. "Is that so? Judgy how?"

"Making assumptions. He's nothing like what I imagined." He smirks a bit. "So, you gonna let me in?"

"You're not dead," he tells me. "Just got grazed with a ball."

133

I blink, and a dull throb beats in my head. Murky green eyes stare back at me.

"You're not Peter?"

"No, I'm Declan."

It takes a minute for things to fall into place. We're at a baseball game. Of the top ten places I never thought I'd go, I was pretty sure a baseball game neared the top of the list. But, I was loving it. The excitement. The thrills. The being close to Declan. And then something thwacked me in the head.

Carefully, I sit up, and realize I'm no longer in the sunlight with the breeze playing in my hair. I'm in a claustrophobic medical room on an exam table. "Well that was embarrassing," I say, swinging my legs off the side.

Declan smirks, stepping between my knees to place his hands on my cheeks, searching my eyes for something important. "Your pupils aren't dilated. That's good."

"Your eyes are really spectacular," I tell him. "Ironically, they're the color of an avocado."

He laughs a little, gingerly fingering my temples. "No, they aren't."

After a few more tests, ibuprofen, and a little while of observation, Declan and the team doctor are convinced I have no lasting damage nor a concussion, and I'm set free.

"Minus the medical room, did you have fun?" he asks me when we drive away.

I smile wide. "I did."

"I had one more surprise, but maybe we shouldn't."

"We should," I encourage, having no idea what the surprise is. I just want to enjoy more time with him. "You said I'm fine, and I feel fine."

His tongue peeks out to wet his bottom lip and then he grins. "Ok."

He drives off into the Hills. Yes, those Hills. Beverly Hills. Twenty minutes later, we are let through a steel gate and continue toward a colossal crescent-shaped mansion. It's striking rubble stoned exterior holds more windows than five of my house.

"Where are we?"

As if it's no big deal, he says, "I'd like you to meet a few of my friends."

"Friends?" My stomach does this weird drop like we just drove down a steep incline instead of a blacktopped circular drive. I don't know if I can do friends. I'm used to being a loner, shut off inside my head. "My hair is a mess."

Declan reaches for my hand and brings it to his lips. "You look perfect."

This is not the time for false compliments. He hops out and before I can lock the doors, he opens mine. Instead of going to the imposing slate gray door, he grabs my hand and navigates around the side of the house to the expansive backyard where there's a pool with a rock waterfall and a lavish spread of food. And lots of people staring as we draw closer. And smiling. Lots of smiling going on.

A dark haired boy with an impish grin runs up to us. "You're pretty."

"Why thank you." I smile at him. "I'm Rose."

"I'm Cooper. Are you and the doc getting married?"

I glance over at Declan who looks unphased by his question. "Umm, no. We're not."

"Ah, it must be the s-e-x," he spells out the word, and then his wise little self darts away, leaving me wishing it wasn't just sex with Declan. That I had never asked him to help me, and just let it happen organically. Because, I want so much more than just s-e-x.

So much more.

———

SOMETIMES WHEN YOU least expect it, you meet people who are...*your people.* And sometimes they quickly become like family.

I've been here a mere three hours, and in that time, I have found my people. People I could see myself hanging out with for the rest of my life.

Chelsea, Nova, and Cat are probably three of the coolest women I've ever met. Besides Julie.

Even Declan's guy friends are all so perfect, hovering about their women, giving them an intimate glance or touch whenever they're nearby. They're a tight knit group, and not once have they made me feel unwelcome.

It's comfortable, like I've known them forever, sitting with them outside at the patio table, while the guys are huddled in the kitchen.

"I like the way he stares at you," Chelsea says, before taking a sip of wine. "I've never seen him like this before."

"Well, I don't think it's like that."

"It's exactly like that," Nova says, pulling out her phone. "I need some books for the flight back to Montana. I hate flying."

You know how you get that prickle at the nape of your neck, like something bad is about to happen? I've got that. And then my worst nightmare happens.

"Get something dirty," Chelsea leans in, animated, "You'll forget all about the flight."

"Ohh this might be good," Cat adds, scooting closer to look at Nova's phone, "*Love Doctor*."

First, good to know my book is showing up in the search. Second, how did I ever think any of this would work? If I were writing a character who is doing what I've done, I'd kill me off.

"Might be a little weird since Declan is a doctor," Nova debates, then looks at me. "No offense."

For a moment, I think she means because I wrote it, but then I realize she means something else entirely. "Oh, none taken," I assure her, my cheeks blushing a little. I've never been so happy to lose a sale.

"There you are," Declan calls out, stepping from the patio door. "We should get going."

Yes, because as much I like these people, my teetering house of cards is about to come tumbling down. I have to tell him. Soon. Maybe.

I rise from my chair, and Chelsea and I exchange phone numbers before we say goodbye to everyone. The ride home is mostly silent, and I sit stoic, watching the palm trees pass by in a blur.

"Everything ok?" he asks with a furrowed brow when he pulls into the parking lot of my building.

I nod. "Yeah." But it's not. Not at all.

Everything about today was beautifully perfect. Except the hit to the head. Maybe not that. But, there's a weight bearing down on me,

"You sure?" he asks again.

I turn to face him. "Declan, your friends were great. The ballpark was great. It was all so…"

"Great?"

"Sorry." It's times like these, I wish I had my thesaurus. "But, it's true. You have so many things going for you, and I…"

"Well, there is one thing I'm missing," he interrupts.

"What's that?"

"You."

Before I can respond, his lips are on mine, erasing every reason I have not to do this. Making me think foolish things, like maybe I could more than like him.

25

Declan

Studies show that most doctors who quote studies are just making up their findings.

NO-STRINGS, she said. A sex study on no-strings relationships, or friends with benefits, whatever you want to call it, showed that sixty nine percent of women were really hoping it turned into strings and sixty percent of men were fine with no strings. Well, count me in the forty percent who isn't. Because what the fuck? There's strings, oh there's strings. Yesterday with Rose was amazing, better than anything I'd ever had before. And the crazy thing is, I want it more now. I thought having her once would cure me of this need for her, thought it would drive her out of my system, but I'm realizing that's not the case.

"Fore," I yell into the vast emptiness of the fairway, even though there's no one around on the golf course except me and Ethan.

I love playing golf. And I love playing with myself. That sounds so dirty, but it's true. Mainly because it's a competition with yourself. No people you're trying to win against. It's all about beating your last score and doing your best. I've been a scratch golfer as long as I can remember, picking up the sport when I was a kid, mainly because it was the best way to spend time with a busy father who never really had time for anything.

It's a clear day, not a single cloud in the sky, and I'm golfing with Ethan. Life is good.

"I can't believe I convinced you to come out here again. Remember what happened last time?" Ethan says from the golf cart, legs perched on the dash, aviator shades low over his eyes.

I line up my Titleist Pro V1 golf ball between the two black tees on the teeing ground for a do over.

"That wasn't my fault." I raise my driver in the air, pointing it at Ethan. "Maybe if you weren't some hot shot movie star you wouldn't be the cause of unwanted attention." I bring my driver back down, pull my arms back, and right before I swing Ethan lets out a 'jealous' which makes me almost miss my shot. Almost.

"Nice try." I wait for him to meet me out here so he can take his shot. "Your turn."

He leans forward, and smiles. "Let's just pretend I drive the ball to somewhere around where your ball landed."

"Get your ass out of that cart and swing."

He laughs, grabbing a driver from his golf bag. "Calm down, I don't want to hear you cry when I beat your ass today." He puts his white tee in the ground, and places his ball on top.

"What's with you today? You drag me out here to not play?"

"Late night with Nova. That girl does this one move," he shakes his head. "I don't know where she gets the energy."

"Man, I don't want to hear about your sex life." I step back, giving him room to swing.

He gets in position. "Just thought we should have a man to man talk." Ethan hits the ball, sending it straight down the fairway.

"Oh, when is the other man arriving?"

"I see you get your sense of humor from your sister." He

rests his weight on the club, hand on hip. "You happy about New York?"

"Yeah." I rub the back of my neck. I should be ecstatic. I should be jumping for joy, this is what I've always wanted, but it feels hollow. Like something's not quite right. Rose has my head so all over the place it isn't funny.

Ethan makes his way to the golf cart and I follow.

"What does Rose think about you taking the job?"

"She's all for it. Can't wait to get rid of me."

Ethan sits down, resumes his position with his feet propped up along the dashboard of the golf cart. "Now, this I need to hear."

And I spill it all to him. Every little thing. Except minor details made only for me. I wouldn't kiss and tell, so I leave it at that.

And when I'm done, he lets out one single, 'fuck.'

I drive us to the next hole. "Yeah, I know."

"Well," Ethan stands from the cart when I come to a stop. "Tell her how you feel."

"And just how do I feel?"

He raises a brow. "Come on. It's obvious."

"Obvious to you. What?" I ask, not sure what he's getting at. "I can't just ask her to go with me."

Ethan leans against the cart, his arms along the top rail, leaning in to glare at me. "That's the stupidest fucking shit I've ever heard. Of course, you can."

My head is all over the place, not really sure which way is up or down. I don't know what's worse—the fact she's a preacher's daughter, my assistant, or the fact I'm wrapped so tight in strings, I'm strangling.

⊏⊐

ROSE and I have been inseparable for the past week, and those strings are now a noose. I don't know how I can leave her. How am I supposed to pick up and move to New York?

Tracy, one of the nurses on duty at the clinic, stares at me from the opposite end of the long desk. It's late in the day, and all I can think about is what Rose and I will be doing later this evening after work.

"What?" I ask.

"Nothing," she says, looking back at her computer screen.

A few minutes later, I catch her staring again. I've known Tracy a long time, and the fact she isn't telling me about some detail of her life is unusual.

I stuff a hand inside my slack's pocket. "Last chance to say whatever's on your mind."

She darts around the desk and stops in front of me to whisper, "I've been reading a book, and I'd swear it's about you."

"What do you mean?" I lean against the desk, curious. "What book?"

Her fingers trace along the wide black band of her ID badge. "*Doctor Love.*"

"Ok, and?" I laugh a little. "I take it this is one of your romance novels? Am I as handsome as in real life?"

"I'm serious," she emphasizes, "and Bonnie and Jackie agree with me. Eclan Bigcock."

"Wait. What?"

"I found this story online," she explains. "And I swear it's you."

She goes on to tell me how Eclan Bigcock is a veterinarian rather than a therapist but fits my description: over six feet, dark blonde, moss-green eyes.

"Let me see this nonsense," I tell her, completely confused.

She grabs her iPhone and swipes the screen. After a few taps, she hands it over. I read the brief description of *Doctor Love*:

Eclan Bigcock—a sexy veterinarian saving the world one pussy at a time. With his panty dropping smile and tug-worthy hair, this alpha male makes all the kitties purr.

I take one look at the cover of the book, a man in a white coat with his chest and abs on display.

"Seriously? What doctor practices medicine with no shirt on?" This is not me. My hair is too short to tug. If anything it should say scratchable muscular back.

"Just read it," she urges.

I let out a beleaguered sigh and continue reading.

He doesn't know I exist. To him, I'm only the owner of the pussy he takes care of.

"Hi," I manage to get out, entering the exam room. Miss Smitten meows in my arms.

Green scrubs emphasize the moss color of his eyes when our gazes meet. "What's going on today?"

His brusque attitude doesn't help ease my nervousness being around him. I've heard the nurses whispering about 'Doctor Love' while I stroke my pussy in the waiting area. I need to get laid.

I stop reading and hand the phone back to Tracy. "What is this garbage?"

"It's you."

"No. I'm not a vet." She opens her mouth to object but reconsiders when she sees how unamused I am. "Who wrote this?"

She shrugs. "It's a pen name, but it has to be someone you know."

"I'm nothing like that guy. I'm not brusque."

Tracy laughs. "There was that one time..."

I put my hand up, stopping her before she continues. "I was tired, and I didn't blow up that bad." She hits me with a stare. "Ok, maybe the one time. But it's not like an everyday occurrence."

She raises a brow. "This book is you."

"Where do I find it?" Because now I'm curious about Eclan Bigcock.

"It's on all the major retailers." She jots down the title and author and hands it over.

I stuff it into my pocket and get back to work. For the rest of the day, I forget all about the vet with the abs.

After work, I meet Rose for dinner at an intimate Italian restaurant.

Dinner is spaghetti and horniness. I've never been around someone who makes me so damn horny. It's like I can't even function when she smiles over her glass of Merlot.

What is she doing to me?

And how am I supposed to leave all this.

I need to talk to her about the job, about moving to New York. It's still a month away, but we need to discuss it. Like yesterday, when Dr. Nicholson brought in the new therapist who will replace me, Rose pretended it didn't even happen.

Maybe she's in denial? Maybe we both are.

"Rose," I start, during dessert, "we should talk about me moving to New York."

The carefree smile, that was there moments ago, drops. "What is there to talk about?"

"Well," I rub my hands on my linen napkin in my lap, "I don't really know, but I think we should at least acknowledge it."

She picks at her tiramisu with her fork. "It's acknowledged."

"We can't hide from it." I blow out a breath. "And what about us?"

She smiles, but it doesn't reach her eyes. "Let's just take it day-by-day."

I hate that idea. But, I hear myself say 'ok' instead.

26

Rose

"I think the deeper you go into questions, the deeper or more interesting the questions get. And I think that's the job of art."
   —*Andre Dubus III*

IT'S ALARMING how comfortable I'm getting around Declan. How comfortable *this* is becoming. We've been complete professionals the past few weeks as he integrates Doctor Beckman into the office. He's been busy, getting ready for his impending move, leaving me alone just enough to miss him. Friday afternoon, at six p.m., he was mine again. And all night long last night, he showed me how much he missed me too.

   I can't imagine once he's really gone and I don't have immediate access to him. Sure we can fly across the country, if life doesn't get in the way. But what's more alarming, is the actual alarm going off—the fire alarm.

   I kick back the comforter wrapped around my body and jump out of bed, slipping on my gray shorts and white tee.

   When I get to the kitchen, Declan, his pants hanging low off his hips, curses at a frying pan filling the space above the stove with smoke. He rushes to the fire alarm, fanning it with his hands.

Trying not to laugh, I cross the tile to open the window above the sink. "Everything ok?"

"Fuck." He steps over to the pan. "Why are my pancakes not coming out right?"

"Well, did you wait for the bubbles to appear?"

He turns to face me, his green eyes narrowed with confusion. "Bubbles?"

I glance into the pan, and oh my. Batter clumps in little balls of goo. There are no pancakes here. "What have you done?"

"I figured pancakes have one ingredient. Add water to the mix, and viola: pancakes. Easy."

I laugh. "It's not that easy, huh?"

"No." He leans in to give me a kiss, moving the batter around as if he's making scrambled eggs.

"How about I make some french toast?" I offer.

He smiles. "Good idea."

"I can teach you how to make them?" I bump his hip with mine.

He holds up his hands, spatula still gripped tightly between his fingers. "I don't know. I'm not much of a cook."

"It's ok. French toast is easy." I open the cupboards looking for the vanilla extract. "I just need to find my vanilla."

"Vanilla? What's that a flower?"

"Vanilla is the most important part of french toast."

Declan raises a brow. "I thought bread was."

"Well, that too." I wink, bumping his hip again to give me a little room to create my masterpiece. "The trick is what kind of bread to use. I grab the bread from the counter, holding it up. "And I have cinnamon loaf."

"Oh, you're serious about your french toast."

I laugh. "I sure am."

For the next few minutes, I teach Declan how to mix the

eggs, milk, and vanilla into a bowl, then together, we dip the bread slices and place them in a new pan.

"You're right. Much easier than pancakes."

"And it'll taste better too." I smile as his arms wrap around me from behind.

"I'm sure it will." He kisses the back of my neck, then moves to the spot just below my ear. It's weird to have someone to share these trivial things with. It's very couple-like. And if we're being honest, I hate the no-strings thing. He's the only man I can see having a lasting future with, and I have this bone-deep urge to ask him to stay. To not go to New York. Or, to take me with him. But, I'll never say those words to him. That's definitely strings, and I know that's not what he wants.

After breakfast is done, Declan has calls to make, because he's flying out early in the morning to New York to look at places to live, and I grab my laptop to check my sales. Twenty total. Clearly I can't fly across the country on the regular from writing. I can't even drive on that. The book has been published for a little while now, and I received my first review yesterday. It says my sex scenes set their fingers on fire. They even used fire emojis.

I have one fan, and I love this flame fingered goddess. Like want to find her and tell her how happy she just made me.

I'd like to tell Declan about it, but the excuses just keep piling up in my brain. Besides, I don't want to tell him about how it's not selling. It's a lot to put on the line and tell people you wrote a book that is failing. So much pressure. So many excuses. I set my laptop aside and decide, I'm going to tell him.

"Hey," he says, returning to the living room. "Sorry to rush out, but I have to go to the clinic today. They're under staffed."

Well, guess I'll tell him later. "Ok, no problem."

He kisses me before leaving, and I stare at the closed door for a few minutes.

Today I stop hiding. I need to put my big girl panties on and be the adult I am. Declan was right about not hiding, and if I can't start with him, I'm going to start with my parents. Even if they're not happy about it, at least I can say I'm being honest.

So, I call my mother and ask to meet her for lunch. Just her. Not my father. Baby steps.

She agrees, and I stand at the mirror, checking my outfit—lemon yellow sundress, denim jacket, and brown ankle boots—for the last time before I leave. Stalling, basically. I slip my glasses on, just to have something to hide behind.

On the drive to Hidden Gems restaurant, I remind myself it's the fear of the unknown that's the worst. And if I don't do this now, I might never do it.

I pull into the lot, park and take a deep breath before heading inside. None of these people eating and chatting at the tables scattered about know my life is about to change. I spot my mother's cinnamon hair at a table near the back.

"Hey, Mom." I take a seat across the table from her. "Thank you for meeting me."

"So formal. Is everything ok?" A worry line forms between her brows.

"Yes, yes. Everything is fine."

The server arrives, and I really have no appetite, so I order a salad, which means I must be *really* nervous.

"So...do you want to explain?" she asks when we're alone.

"Mom, remember when I was young, and I would write stories all the time?"

She smiles. "Yes. I remember that one particular story about the dragon who burned down the bakery because they had no cookies that got you in trouble."

I remember that too. Dad took away television for two weeks even though I had made sure everyone inside got out safely. I take a deep breath, and let it out ever so slowly. "Well, I still write. I published a book. About sex."

My mother's water glass stops on the way to her lips. "Come again?"

I take a sip of my soda. "Sex, Mom."

"Like *Fifty Shades Of Grey?*"

"No." I shake my head. "Well, sort of. Not the BDSM stuff, but there is sex in my books, Mom. Premarital sex."

She takes a slow sip of water. "Ah, I see." She doesn't speak for a few hour-like moments.

Her face looks a little pale next to the navy of her blouse, and I'm about ready to ask if she's ok when we're interrupted by the server bringing our salads. I thank him, and once he's left the table, I peek over at my mother whose eyes haven't left my face.

"Mom?"

"I'm trying to process it." Process is good. That means she's not totally opposed to the idea. "Why didn't you say anything before now?"

I push the lettuce around in my bowl. "Well, I didn't want to disappoint you. You never seemed to approve of the writing." I look up at her. "But this is what I want to do. And I'm going to."

Her gray eyes are solemn. "You're my baby, Rose. That was a long time ago, and really, I didn't know what I was doing back then. It's a lot of trial and error." She sighs and leans across the table a bit. "Want to know a secret?"

"Sure."

"I read *Fifty Shades Of Grey.*"

"You did?" I can't believe my own ears.

She nods, and with a hint of laughter in her voice, shocks me, "I've read quite a few racy books."

"Mom, you're so naughty."

She swats at my hand, her cheeks turning a bright shade of crimson. "Oh, stop." Then her expression becomes serious. "And don't tell your father."

I do the motion of zipping up my lips and throwing away the key. "I won't say a word."

She asks about my book, and I tell her as we finish our lunch. Then I clean the rest of the slate by telling her Declan is a sex therapist. And we're involved. And he's leaving.

My poor mom takes it much better than I expected. "Rose, I don't expect you to be a saint. They're your choices to make. I don't know if we can choose who we love, I think that's unavoidable, but you can choose whether you're with them or not."

"Why does being an adult have to be so hard?"

She laughs. "It only gets worse."

We finish up our lunch, and I feel a slight burden has been lifted when I leave. Mom is human just like me, and maybe if I spent less time in my head, I would've seen that. She's an ally, not an enemy. Instead of going home right away, I stop at the bookstore and browse the aisles for hours until I get a text from Declan that he's finishing up his shift.

For some reason, the thought of telling Declan is scarier than my parents—which is probably why I started with my mom—but I'm going to do it.

Maybe I'm a sex addict? Because when I arrive home and see him waiting outside my door in worn jeans and a simple black T-shirt, I don't think about tomorrow, or the future, or my book. Instead, I walk to him like a junkie needing a fix and rise on my tiptoes to kiss his sensual lips.

He charges through the front door like a bull in the streets of Pamplona and slams it shut with his foot. And he almost growls at me as he sets me down, his hand connecting with my ass.

"I need this," he groans, my ass still in the grip of his hand.

He's created a monster; I really must be a sex addict, because I love this new savage beast side of him. This can't be normal to have this much sex. To remove your clothes right in your entryway, like I just did.

He marches me to the back bedroom, and flings me onto the bed, and I land with a little bounce.

Like a tiger about to pounce, he moves up the bed, over me, on top of me. I want to tell him all the things, but like some demented heroine who can't get her shit together, and makes my eyes roll out of my head, I make another bad choice and don't.

27

Declan

Having studied Human Anatomy for many years in school, doctors are well-versed in the art of love making. This fact is completely made up.

I'VE NEVER BEEN SO greedy, or hard, or so close to coming undone in all my life. Everytime I think I can't take another second of her, she smiles, or draws her hand over my chest, or moves the slightest bit to where I could possibly combust.

I can feel the need taking over. The need to fuck, push my dick in, tighten my grip on her.

I want to take this slow, but fuck, how can I? How can I take things at a snail's pace when this woman stares at me the way she does? Like she's the needier between the two of us.

Not fucking possible.

And in this moment, I know I'm completely crazy for this girl.

I work my way up her body, licking, kissing, sucking, nibbling, fucking making love to her sweet, sultry skin with my lips. She cries out my name when I press my mouth to her pussy, dipping my tongue inside. I am in-fucking-satiable for her.

"Touch yourself, Rose," I tell her.

Her back arches, her knees slipping further apart, and I'm right here, taking it all in as she runs a hand over her pussy, her confidence never wavering. And it's fucking sexy.

"Is that where you want me?" I ask her.

She nods, biting her lower lip.

I slip on a condom before I thrust long and slow inside her, filling her to the hilt with my cock, loving the visual of my dick sliding in and out of her. I lean back, spreading her legs just a bit more, so I can watch as her pussy owns me. It's next level with her, and I try my best to not be consumed by thoughts of forever and happiness, and stay in the here and now, but it's hard when I see the dimple that surfaces when she smiles ever so slightly. Or the hint of freckles scattered across her nose. God, how I love those fucking freckles.

Thundering through the onslaught of emotions rising from deep within me, from places I never knew I possessed, I kiss her through our orgasms. I kiss her as my mind begs me to say those three little words I've never said to any woman. Words that scare the fuck out of me. Words that keep me awake long after she falls asleep curled into me. Since I can't sleep, I pull up the book site on my phone and search for *Doctor Love*. This book has me questioning a little. Eclan Bigcock is too much of a coincidence. While Rose sleeps, I purchase the book, prop up a little, and head off to chapter one. And before I know it I'm sucked into the book.

Like I can't believe I'm reading a romance novel. And it's not because the storyline is riveting, it's, hmm…familiar.

It isn't until I come to a scene where Eclan fingers the heroine in a nightclub that I really take notice. I keep reading, glancing over at a sleeping Rose with her hand tucked under her cheek, wondering why my sexual experiences with her are in this book.

Did she tell someone all this? Something tugs at my brain

and then I back track to a scene and re read it. It's the one Rose had me read in my office.

Did she write this?

I finish reading off the story, in full confusion over a few more scenes that play out just like with Rose and me.

Why?

I mean, it's obvious she wrote these words. And if she didn't write them, then she obviously told someone about our sex. And the thought makes me feel used. I feel like the biggest lie in this place. Like I was used as a pawn in a much bigger scheme. Maybe I'm making too big of a deal about this, but it's not everyday I fall in love.

It's not any day, actually. This is a first for me.

Even now, being this close to her has my heart in an outrage. Has it beating this uneasy tempo. Part of me wants to kiss her and wake her, but the other part wants to walk away and never look back.

Quietly, I slip out of bed, get dressed and before I leave, I cut the strings and place the ereader on the pillow next to her. And then, because there's one thread still clinging, I kiss her gently on the forehead before I walk out.

28

Rose

"Writing is an exploration. You start from nothing and learn as you go."
—E. L. Doctorow

THIS IS BAD. I woke to an empty bed and no sign of Declan. When I picked up the e-reader on his pillow, the light came on. And then I sat on the edge of the bed in disbelief. And that's where I still sit, still in disbelief. Pru ripped off my book. And Declan was reading it.

She didn't only steal my title and have the balls to make it *Doctor Love* instead of *Love Doctor*, she used my sex scenes from the critique group. I can't even feel my face. Oh god, she kept the name Eclan Bigcock. I changed mine to Gabriel. I changed it all to hide it was Declan. I didn't use any of these scenes in *Love Doctor*.

Even though I know he's probably thirty thousand feet in the air, I grab my phone from the nightstand and text him. He doesn't answer.

Julie is my next text. "Can you come over? Now."

"Yeah. What's up?" she replies.

"I'll explain when you get here."

"Be there in fifteen."

While I wait, I skim back through. She did add one of her own scenes. She's got Eclan in a threesome. I guess this is my retribution. What must he have thought being blindsided with this? I wallow in my misery until Julie arrives.

"What's going on?" she asks as soon as I open the door.

Her expression ranges from shocked to dismayed as I tell her what happened. She follows me into the living room, and I grab my laptop from the coffee table before plopping down beside her on the couch.

Then I pull up the bookstore website and...oh my god, Pru's book is a bestseller. Even the cover is a rip off.

"Look." I thrust the computer so Julie can see what I'm seeing.

"Oh no she didn't," Julie bites out, eyeing the copy of her work.

"I can't believe this…" my words catch in my throat. Tears well in my eyes, hovering, threaten to spill over, but I won't cry over this.

Rebecca was right. This really is how Pru releases so fast. She steals other people's stories with no shame.

"There has to be something we can do," Julie says. "I know people."

"I didn't copyright my chapters I let everyone read."

"Probably wouldn't have mattered," she says.

A tear finally escapes, racing down my cheek. "Declan read it."

"What?" Julie's mouth drops open. "What did he…"

I wipe the tear away, but another quickly follows. "I haven't talked to him. He was flying to New York this morning and was gone when I woke up. He left the e-reader on his pillow."

Julie's arm reaches around my shoulders, and she pulls me in for a hug. "Shh. It's ok. We'll fix this. No one knows it's him."

"But she used that name."

"First things first, you need to call Pru."

I don't like this industry where people steal things and profit. I don't want to be an author anymore. But I want to make sure I'm smart about this. I want to make sure I have all my ducks lined in a neat little row, before I make a move.

29

Declan

Medical doctors are just as likely to abuse alcohol just like the rest of us. This fact is not made up.

SOMETIMES YOU HAVE to drink your problems away.

Instead of flying to New York to meet with the real estate agent, I changed my flight to tomorrow. Who really needs a place to live when you're Eclan Bigcock? I'll just hang out under my big cock. Maybe I'll just become a porn star. Nah, I'd need a fluffer and I'd need it to be Rose. And then I'd just fuck *her* all day.

I want to call her. But, I don't know what to say yet. Is that what the no strings was about? Was all the sex for a sequel?

"Jonah, what's up?" I slur a little as he slides on the stool next to me at the sports bar where I've set up shop.

"Well, you asked me to meet you. You ok?"

How do I even answer that question right now? Am I ok? No, I'm very much not ok. What I am is Eclan Bigcock. Handler of pussies.

But, I don't give him that weighted answer. "Yeah, man. I'm fine."

Jonah being Jonah sees right through my bullshit. "You don't look so fine."

"Oh, what are you? A doctor now?" I'll admit I'm in a bad mood. And I know I shouldn't be taking it out on him, but he's the one here right now. So, lucky him. "Doctor Love? Is that your name?" I hold my glass up for a cheers. "Eclan Bigcock. Nice to meet you."

"Dude," his dark brows pull together, "what the hell are you talking about?"

I swivel on my stool to face him, my finger wagging in his face, and for the first time in a long time, I tell him exactly how I feel. For so long in my life, I've always been the listener. Being a therapist, it's always come easy for me. But, I purge everything and it feels damn good.

"She wrote the book?" he asks me.

I shrug. "Not sure."

"Well, I think you should at least find that out."

My phone vibrates in my pocket, and I pull it out. Another text from Rose lights up my screen in the dimly lit bar.

"It's her," I say to Jonah. "She wants to explain."

"Go talk to her. It'll drive you crazy if you don't. I'll drop you off."

I finish off my beer and follow Jonah to his Jeep. Chances are, if I go to her house, I won't be able to think straight. Not because I'm drunk, which I am, but because she's more intoxicating than any top shelf liquor I could ever consume. She makes my veins burn. And Eclan Bigcock can not have burning veins. I hold up a finger to Jonah beside his Jeep and pull my phone out to dial her number, swaying just a bit as I do.

She answers on the first ring. "I didn't write the book, but I know who did," she says in a remorseful tone.

"Who?"

"It's a girl named Pru Palmer, and she's in a writing group

with me. I went there while working on my own novel, *Love Doctor*. It wasn't about us, or anything. But, I was writing scenes that you were helping me with—sexy scenes. And well, she stole them. I never meant anything to come of it. But, she's just a horrible person and well…"

I rub a hand over my stubbled chin.

"You're a writer?" But more important, "Was that angry sex note yours?"

"Um," Jonah cringes a little before opening his door, "I'll just wait in the Jeep."

"Yes, but as Ruby Red." Ah, fitting. "And yeah it was. You made me really mad about that muffin," she informs me, "because I was attracted to you and didn't want to be."

This is why I can't go over there, because angry sex. I need distance. And lots of it. Although, I *am* Eclan Bigcock, I'm sure I could reach her from here. I wobble a bit on my feet and brace my hand on the Jeep. Seems like there's something important I need to know. Oh right, "What about the sessions, Rose? Did you ask for my help to help you write sex scenes?"

"Yes, I did." Regret pervades her soft voice. "But, it wasn't a lie. I really was inexperienced and wanted to know more."

I shake all the memories of us together from my head. "I broke so many rules for you. All so you could use it as filler in your novel?"

"No," she adamantly denies. "It was so much more than that. You made me more confident in my writing. You helped me."

"Well, I'm glad I could do that for you."

"Declan…"

"Rose, it doesn't matter." The real issue is one she can't write a happy ending for. "I'm leaving tomorrow. I just have a few last-minute things I need to get together."

"You're not there in New York?"

"Nope. I was thirsty, so I decided to drink the bar."

"I'm sorry," she says, quietly. "You have to understand."

"I do understand." It's her who doesn't understand. She'll be here, and I'll be there, and that's really what matters.

"We can talk when you get back," she says in a voice that makes me want to go over there. The parking lot swirls around me, and I tell her goodbye, climb in the Jeep and pass the fuck out.

———

NEW YORK IS GREAT. It's as great as great can get. And although it's great, I try my hardest to pretend this void inside me isn't there. It's like a black hole growing larger every second. Maybe if I say great again. New York is fucking *great*.

Nope. It doesn't help.

As I walk through the spacious luxury apartment on Fifth Ave, I have this one fantasy I keep replaying over and over in my mind. It's of Rose and I, living in this apartment, her tapping away on a keyboard. Me, reading in my lounger, watching her.

"I'll take it," I tell the realtor.

She smiles, pulling out her Montblanc pen. "I thought you'd like this one."

Something doesn't feel right. And it may never feel right. I walk across the light oak hardwoods in the living room to the wall of glass and look out on the bustling city of millions. All these people and the one I want is in LA.

30

Rose

"Either write something worth reading or do something worth writing."
  —*Benjamin Franklin*

"I NEED you to get me a miracle," I tell my father in his office after the Sunday evening filming of his show.

His confused gray eyes narrow on me standing before his desk. "It doesn't exactly work that way."

I'm desperate. Desperate enough that I sit down and proceed to tell my father about my writing, my book, and Declan. "I'm sorry to shock you with this. But I'm an adult now, and I have faults. And you can't exactly give me away, so we'll have to meet in the middle." I choke back a sob. "I really need that miracle."

He rises, crossing around the desk and envelopes me in comfort while I cry. "I'll see what I can do."

It feels like another weight has been lifted by getting this out in the open. "We all have faults," he remarks, when my tears subside. "You should have more faith in love, Rose."

"It's hard to trust something you can't see," I tell him.

He leans back a bit and grabs a tissue from the holder on his desk. "But do you feel it?" I nod, wiping my eyes. "Then it's there."

For someone who writes romance, I sure don't know what I'm doing. His assistant knocks and lets him know it's time to go over some business for the show.

"I'll be right there," he informs him.

I stand, and before I leave him to finish up his business, he pulls me in for another reassuring embrace. "I'll be talking to my attorney for you," his tone leaves no room for argument, "because although we should turn the other cheek at times, this isn't one of them."

I smile and give him a squeeze.

On my way home to mope, my miracle comes in an unexpected form—Chelsea Sincock.

I pull into a mini mart lot to take her call.

"Jonah told me about what happened with you and my brother," she says after I greet her. "So I bought your book, the right one, and I did a thing."

"A thing?"

"Well, I loved it, so I wanted people to know. So I did a post about it."

I sit up straight in my seat, stunned. "Thank you, Chelsea." I don't even know how to thank her, or better yet what I can do to repay her. Or why she would do this. And then I ask about what I care about most, "How is Declan?"

"Well, he's Declan. I'm a firm believer in love, and you two are meant to be. And none of that changes my opinion of your book. I really did love it. And the scenes were on fire."

I smile. "Thank you." And then my smile fades, because well, I don't have *him*.

We chat for a few more minutes and she makes me promise we will get together soon. After we hang up, I pull up the internet on my phone and find Chelsea's post about *Love Doctor.*

Not only has Chelsea shared my book, she's told them not to confuse it with the fake.

Thousands of people have commented, saying they just bought it. I can't believe the hype and buzz I see about my book being created by Chelsea. I like her video, and comment with a thank you and a million crying emojis. For all the bad like Pru, there's good like Chelsea.

I pull up my sales and whoa—whoa—the sales number is staggering. It all feels a little hollow, though, because of how it all came to be.

Maybe I should go to New York to see him? Tell him how I feel about him.

I want to be with Declan, more than I've ever wanted anything else in my life. So, even if this is me declaring my love for a man who may not love me back, I have to take that chance. It may be heartbreaking, it may crush my soul, but I have to at least try. Because, well, you never know. My mind is made up. While I sit in the mini mart lot, with people filtering in and out, I decide I'm going to New York. If I were writing this novel, she wouldn't give up. No one wants to read about that. No, she'd run through the airport right before his plane takes off, or hold a boombox over her head and play his favorite song, or ride up to him in a white limo with flowers in hand to declare her love. My whole life I've always done what others expected of me. And now I know that's not necessary. And then I do what's really unexpected...I unpublish my novel.

31

Declan

"Observation, Reason, Human Understanding, Courage; these make the physician."
———*Martin H. Fischer*

HAVE I mentioned that just because my sister is a famous movie star doesn't mean she's not annoying? On the flight home to LA, my conversation with her on the way to the airport kept finding its way back in my head.

"Wait, the girl you fell for wrote a book about having sex with you...and that's a bad thing?"

"Well, she lied to me."

"Would you have helped her had she told you the truth?"

"Probably. Maybe. I don't know."

"I can't believe you've fallen for a romance novelist. Have you read her book?"

"No, but I'm sure it's good. And I'm not just saying that because I'm in love with the girl or anything."

"Mhm."

And then I realized I *am* in love with Rose.

And I said it again in my mind just to hear it, and it didn't sound crazy or wrong.

"Well, does any of it matter? I mean, you'll be living in New York, her in Cali. Unless you do something about it. Just sayin.'"

See, annoying. So, once the plane took off, I ended up pulling up the ebook store and did a quick search of *Love Doctor.* I scrolled through the abs and stopped on Ruby Red and purchased the book. And now I can't stop reading. I've read it all in one-sitting, laughing along as Annette falls in love with her boss. Who is much better than Eclan Bigcock, I might add. I'm a little in awe of Rose right now.

When I land at the LAX airport, I hail a cab to get me to Rose's apartment. The sun has long set over the Pacific Ocean, and I have no idea what I'll say to her when I see her, but I know I can't spend one more miserable day without her.

The palm trees sway as the cab driver cruises through the streets, bringing me closer to her.

He parks by the large bougainvillea bush next to the walkway of her place. A gentle breeze rushes past me as I step from the car. I grab my bag, rush up the stairs, and knock.

She opens the door with a whoosh, looking like an angel in a flowy white sundress. "Declan?" She smiles, faintly. "I was on my way to New York...to find you."

"Why?"

She looks up at me. "Because I love you."

Fuck. The power of those words. "Say it again."

"I love you."

And then I kiss her, long and deep, wrapping my arms around her tiny waist. "I love you too," I murmur against her lips. "I quit the job in New York."

Her eyebrows shoot up with surprise and she pulls back. "You what? Why?"

"Because I love you."

She shakes her head. "You can't quit that job for me. I won't allow it." She's cute when she's all riled up.

"Well, it's too late, because I did."

She shakes her head again. "No, you need to call Dr. Dale, tell him you made a mistake."

I tighten my arm around her waist. "The only mistake I made was not telling you I love you sooner." She gets this love look on her face, and I move in, drawing her lips to mine, kissing her, sliding my tongue between her lips. She opens for me, her tongue meeting mine, and I pull her closer. So damn good. I like kissing her like this. Like when she's mine. And I'm hers. And that's how it will stay, no matter where we end up.

Epilogue

Rose

WHEN I WRITE, I like to leave my characters at their happiest. And if I were writing my story, it would never end. Because every day is the happiest.

We didn't stay in LA long. Just long enough to have a grand send off, and for Declan and I to pack up all my belongings and ship them to New York.

Dr. Houston Dale was very understanding, said he'd done crazy things for love himself, and Declan was able to keep his job.

I thought I'd miss LA, but you know what? I love New York's kick-your-ass vibe. Declan and I haven't even begun to touch all the nooks and crannies.

You're probably wondering what happened with Pru. Well, when we signed up for the class we all signed a contract. I'll be honest, I didn't read the fine print. Turns out, not only was there an NDA, there was also a form that said anything we brought in for the group was protected under a copyright, and no one could, in a sense, steal your scenes. Just like she had.

Christian had all the paperwork I needed, and Declan and I reached out to my father's lawyer, and a few weeks later Pru unpublished her book, *Doctor Love*. But, that was a small blip for her. She's released a zillion more times. I don't care, though. I try my best not to dwell on the negativity. Her misery and jealousy is not something I focus on in my day-to-day life. I'm too busy actually writing and managing my new career.

Declan convinced me to republish *Love Doctor* that night he came to my house, and thanks to Chelsea, it soared up the charts.

Some days I have to pinch myself to make sure this is all real.

Since I've moved to New York, I've published another book —an angst-ridden follow-up to Annette and Gabriel's story. Just because I'm happy, doesn't mean they get to be. I'm a writer after all. No pain, no gain. Love is funny, sometimes you have to be smacked right upside the head with it, like a foul ball at a baseball game.

As embarrassing as that was, I think that was the moment I fell in love with Declan. It was his smirk. That irresistible smirk. And his denial that his eyes are the color of avocados. They so are. See? I could go on and on. He makes me feel like I can conquer the world.

And I kind of feel like I have. Thanks to Chelsea and Nova's support of my books, I'm able to write full-time and have been picked up by a publisher here in the city. My new series is about vampires. In elevators.

"Rose, you home?" Declan calls out as he enters our two-story brownstone.

"Up here," I yell for him.

He rushes up the stairs, entering my little writing studio with long, loose strides and a languid smile, like he has all the time in the world to just stare at me.

"I got this for the dog." He holds out an adorable frog for the husky we're adopting tomorrow.

"She'll love it." I smile. "And it's Thumbelina."

He places it on her bed, grinning. "Yeah." He sits next to me, his hand landing on my knee, squeezing gently. "How was your day?" he asks.

"I was just starting a new story."

"Vampires?"

I bat my lashes at him. "That would be the one."

His hand travels up my thigh, underneath my skirt and even higher still. "Maybe we should practice a few of the sex scenes."

I move closer, draping my arms lightly around his neck. "I think that's a great idea, Dr. Sincock."

He leans in, capturing my lips with his. Every kiss is like the first. The same passion. The same butterflies.

I close my eyes, my face tilting, mouth opening just for him, and let his tongue caress mine.

And then he scoops me up, carrying me out of my little haven, down the hallway decorated with photos of Los Angeles, taken by his friend Jonah, and into our bedroom where all kinds of wicked things take place. And now today replaces yesterday as the happiest. And then tomorrow will replace this one as the happiest, and it will never end.

Extended Epilogue

Declan

There are two-hundred and twenty-two steps from work to my apartment. Steps filled with scattering leaves from a fall evening. Steps where I think to myself, I'm the luckiest man on the planet. Because, well, I am.

It all worked out for me in the end; I have everything I could have ever asked for.

There's a few times over the past few months where I lost hope. I didn't think it would work out, but I never gave up on my dream.

Sure, being a sex therapist was awesome. I like to think in many ways I helped people. And it also led me to Rose, the brightest, sassiest woman I've ever met. Her innocence and boldness is something I treasure daily. I'll let you in on a secret...

Rose was part of my dream.

No, not in a creepy type of way, but in a she's the one kind of way.

After seeing all my friends finding the one, and getting married, I felt like I was being left behind. I didn't want to admit to myself that I was lonely, but I was. So, I threw myself into my work. Into a job I didn't really care for. And after a while, I forgot about the dreams and goals I wanted for myself.

Until the day I found the angry sex note from Rose.

And let me tell you, sometimes I come home to find crazier notes than that on little sheets of paper.

What's better than dating a romance writer? Nothing. The best part is working out the naughty scenes with her. The dirty things she writes on her notes. It's my favorite.

Also, that study was right, redheads do have a thing for kink. And lucky for me, my girl has a wild side.

New York really is ...great.

And I hate to admit it, but Houston was right—I will be inviting him to my wedding.

"There is one thing I still haven't ever done," she says one evening as we sit together in our apartment, lounging on the couch.

"What's that?"

A mischievous smile crosses her face. "Given a..." her words trail off.

I know what she's getting at, and I spread my legs just a bit. "A what?" I want to hear her say the words.

"Blowjob." Her lips are so damn plump, so damn ready for me.

"Yeah?" I run my hand over the bulge growing underneath my pants.

She scoots closer to me. "Yes." She replaces my hand with hers, massaging over my hardened dick before unzipping my pants. There's no mistaking the hunger in her eyes.

She gets on her knees, between my legs, her fingers hooking into my belt loops, and slides my pants down and off. The bulge in my boxer briefs is right at eye level for her, and she licks her lips again.

There's nothing more in the world I want than to shove my

dick deep down her throat. I cup her cheeks with my hands, angling her face to look up at me. "Rose, are you hungry for it?"

"Yes." Her cheeks blush.

My hand tightens my hold on her head, my fingers flying into her wild hair. "Only if you want to, baby." I would never make her do anything she doesn't want to do, including this.

She nods. "I want to. Just make sure you tell me if I'm doing it right."

The teacher, always the teacher with her. I lean my head back, closing my eyes as she pumps her hand around the tip of my dick after ridding me of my boxer briefs, and the sensation throws me into overdrive. I grunt a little as I lean into her touch. "That's right. Now wrap that pretty little mouth of yours around it."

She opens her mouth, sticking her pink tongue out to swipe at the tip of my dick.

I tighten my grip on her wild tresses, groaning at the feel of her breath along my steel-hard cock. "Suck on it, Rose."

Her gaze meets mine, and she runs her tongue from the base of my dick to the top. "Is that what you want?" she asks me.

I nod, unable to answer my girl with coherent words. The anticipation is killing me.

And then shit gets real when she wraps those pretty lips around my dick. She takes it slow, ever so slow, sucking all over me, like she knows what she's doing.

"Are you sure you've never done this before?" I ask

She releases me to answer, "I've seen porn with it."

Ah, fuck. My eyes stay locked with hers, and I thrust back into her mouth. "Keep going, baby."

And she does, sucking and licking, bringing me so close to coming all down her throat.

She picks up speed. It's taking everything in me not to slam as hard as I can into her mouth, fucking her with everything I have.

I replace her hand on my dick with mine. "Just keep your mouth open," I tell her, pumping my cock.

She does it, sticking her tongue out just a bit, and her hands grab my ass. Her nails dig into my skin, and I fuck her beautiful lips.

"I'm going to come," I say just before I fill her hot mouth with my release.

If you would have asked me a year ago where I'd be now, I would have never in a million years pictured this scenario. Sure, I'd hope for it, but I'd never think I'd actually be in love with one of the coolest, funniest, smartest women around.

And hey, that's not a biased opinion. Rose is cool as hell. In fact, she has a thing for having tacos on Thursdays, and she leaves the avocados off just for me, 'cause she knows there's nothing super about them. You know something else she does really good? She loves me with her whole heart. More than I could have ever hoped to be loved.

And I try everyday to show her I love her just as much.

Acknowledgments

Thank you so much for reading this book and taking a chance on me. I hope you enjoyed Declan and Rose's story. It's sad to see the series end, and I've had such a great time bringing the four best friends, Jonah, Booker, Ethan, and Declan to you. I hope you enjoyed their stories as well.

As always, thank you so much to Paula Dawn for all your help and inspiration with this book. Your friendship knows no bounds.

I appreciate you.

Thank you to Keri R., Rachel C., Angie S., Catherine S., Vanessa S., Crystal G., and Vanessa D. for your helpful eyes in reading over the book.

I'd like to thank the lovely ladies of my Facebook Group, Logan Chance's The Dark Side. You ladies are truly one of the best things about being an author.

Thank you to every blogger, and reader who has ever shared, mentioned, recommended, loved, liked, or commented on any of my books. I appreciate your support in all you do. Thank you.

Rose's story hit home for me in many ways. It's a brutal world as an Indie Author, but I love it all the same.

I also wanted to say, a few of the places in California were made up for sake of the story. There is no pier in Santa Maria....that I know of.

Keep reading for a few sneak peeks.

Also, if you want to know more about Houston Dale and Marley, grab their story with STUDY ME, a student/teacher romance available now.

You can find Jonah in PLAYBOY, available now.

You can find Booker in HEARTBREAKER, available now.

You can find Ethan in STUCK, available now.

The PLAYBOY Series

Have you read TAKEN the top 25 Amazon bestselling book? STOLEN, book 2 in the Taken Series will be releasing late Spring 2019.

This is one story you won't want to miss.

Be sure to add it to your Goodreads TBR so you don't miss out on this one: Click Here

And Grab TAKEN today: SHOP NOW

Also releasing this Spring is the SPRING FLING ANTHOL-OGY. 15 bestselling authors are bringing you their hottest spring fling novellas.

FLINGOLOGY by Logan Chance will be featured in this anthology, and you can preorder now at the preorder price of only 99 cents.

Order Now: Pre-Order Now

Playboy (Book One in the PLAYBOY Series)
A Top 100 Amazon Best Seller

Doing this photoshoot with my best friend's little sister is about to get...hard.

They call me a playboy.

Sure, I like to have fun with the opposite sex, but hey, in my line of work, who wouldn't?

My name's Jonah and I work for Bunny Hunnies, a swimsuit magazine. Calling the shots, and taking pictures of gorgeous women is every man's fantasy, including mine.

That is, until Chelsea Sincock walks onto the set of one of my shoots.

I've known Chelsea since before she was this hot as hell vixen wearing nothing but a bikini.

What is she doing here?

Does her brother, Declan, know?

Did I mention he's my best friend?

This is going to be hard, I mean difficult, to work with her. And the more I gaze at her from behind the lens, the more I realize I'm in way over my head.

SHOP NOW

Heartbreaker (Book Two in the PLAYBOY Series)

Here's some advice…

When the sexy new guy in town throws your rock, and steals your favorite chocolate-covered donut, chances are he's bad news.

I hate him. His sexy smirk is one thing I want to banish from my life.

Things have been going so smoothly now for years, I don't need his charm infecting me.

My son and I live a simple life, until the moment Booker Reed hires me to fix up his childhood home's garden.

It doesn't help when I show up each day he's naked. What a jerk.

What a big, sexy jerk. And I do mean big…down there.

But the more I work for him the more his vulnerability gets to me.

It makes my heart ache, and the more I get to know him the more I can't resist. I can't help but fall for him.

The worst part is, he's leaving when the house sells. I almost hope he doesn't leave, but once I learn the truth he just can't stay.

I know I can't afford the heartbreak.

I won't put my son through that either.

But one thing is for certain, I can't ever forget this man who stole not only my donut, but my heart and now threatens to break it.

SHOP NOW

Stuck (Book Three in the PLAYBOY Series)
NOW A TOP 17 AMAZON BESTSELLER

I'm not starstruck. I'm just star...stuck.

It's not everyday you have the number one box office star in your car. Actually, not any day for someone like me, Nova Sparks, a plain Jane hair stylist.

And the real kick in the rear end? Not only will he be in my car, in a few weeks, he'll be in my life— as my stepbrother.

Fate has brought Ethan Hale into my small Montana world and kept him unattainable. How's that for cruel?

Now I'm stuck being near him. Stuck with the tabloids and paparazzi. Stuck with these feelings I shouldn't be having.

The only way to get unstuck is accept I can't have him and send him back to Hollywood.

The only problem? He may have other plans.

SHOP NOW

Sneak Peek TAKEN

TAKEN the top 25 Amazon best seller is currently on SALE for 99 cents, read on for the first chapter.

Chapter One
Rhiannon
Eight years old

"Shh, you'll get us caught."

"No one's going to find us. Don't be such a baby, Rhi."

"I'm not a baby," my voice raises a little with denial.

I hate when Xavier calls me a baby. I'm eight years old and can do a ton of things for myself. Like, daddy lets me ride my bike around the neighborhood all alone. Well, really until the end of the street, but still. Plus, grownups say I have a mature soul; whatever that means. It doesn't sound babyish, though.

"No talking until we get outside," he whispers. He's so bossy. But, he is two years older than me, so I guess, technically, he *is* in charge. Plus, he's my best friend, so I overlook these things.

We duck out the French door in the kitchen, into the dark, trying our best not to make a sound.

This probably isn't a good idea. Rescue the princess is a game we play often but never at night.

The moon plays peekaboo in the cloud-covered sky, and we slip like mist across the damp grass, hopefully without being seen by the guards.

If my father found us sneaking out, we'd probably be murdered. You think I'm exaggerating, but I'm not. I've heard the staff whispering when they think I'm not listening. Once, I asked my mother if he's a bad man, and she told me never to say it again. She said he protects us from the other bad people of the world. So, I guess he's good to us.

Well, good to me, anyways. He doesn't care much for Xavier. Mom says he only tolerates him because he's Hannah's son. She's our maid, tall with beautiful hair the color of chocolate, and one of the nicest women I've ever met. And if I'm being honest, sometimes, when she brushes my long red hair, I pretend she's my mother.

Don't get me wrong, I love my mom, but she's always busy entertaining my dad's boring friends when she's not working at his office.

"This way," Xavier directs, leading me down the uneven cobblestone path that cuts through the backyard.

He grabs my hand when I hesitate, and like always, I feel as if nothing can harm me out here with him.

"We're almost there," he reassures, taking us away from the safety of the big brick house, toward the towering woods.

"Maybe we shouldn't," I hedge.

Unsure, I peek over my shoulder for a moment. Like a beacon calling me home, a light flickers through an upstairs window.

"No turning back." Xavier's blue eyes glow with anticipation of all the things I'm afraid of as he tugs me along. He's the opposite of me: fearless.

A blanket of twigs snap beneath our sneakers as Xavier tightens his grip on my sweaty hand. Crickets chirp and things I don't want to think about rustle through the darkness as we move further than I've ever been through the knotty trunks.

A small cabin, in a clearing, comes into view, and he rushes up the rickety stairs, to the front door, dropping my hand somewhere along the way.

Spooky shadows lurk inside the windows, and I hang back a bit, my sneakers cemented to the earth. "What's in there?"

"Don't be a fraidy cat."

"I'm not afraid." I raise my chin and step on the first wooden plank leading up to a small porch.

He opens the door. "Ready?"

I'm not, but I'll never let him know it, so I continue on and follow him into the unknown.

He flicks his flashlight on and scans the room. The dark walls are bare, and a lone chair sits like a throne in the middle of the room with steel handcuffs attached to both arms.

"What is this place?"

"I don't know," he answers, looking over at me. "I followed your dad and his friends the other day down here."

"Xavier, we shouldn't be here. I don't think good things happen in this place. I don't like it here."

He grabs my arm, his blue eyes holding mine. "One day, I'll take you away from your father and all the bad things."

Xavier has never liked daddy either. His cold hard stare. The gruff in his voice when he yells at him for everything.

My father calls him a ...nuisance.

"What if I don't want to leave?"

"What could you possibly like about living with your father?"

I don't get to answer because there's a snap of a tree branch outside.

"Hide," he says, flicking off his flashlight. We crouch by the far wall of the small cabin, behind a table of tools I don't fully understand.

The front door flies open. "Who's in here?" The sound of

my father's voice startles us both. Xavier, eyes loaded with fear, slaps a hand over my mouth before I can answer.

Tucking my knees to my chest, I try to make myself disappear. I squeeze my eyes shut, anything to make me go away. My father will probably spank me for being out here, maybe ground me forever from playing outside, but it's nothing compared to what he'll do to Xavier.

He might even go so far as to fire his mother.

When my father shines his light around the room, we shrink back into the small alcove of the side. Footsteps fall faster to our hiding spot, and Xavier is yanked up by his hoodie.

"You're hiding like a rat," my father bites out. "Why are you in here?"

Xavier's eyes meet mine, and he gives a little shake of his head, warning me to stay silent. "Answer me," he yells so loud it feels like the walls vibrate.

"I was just exploring," Xavier finally responds.

"Exploring?" My father drags him to the chair and drops him down in it. "Come out of there, Rhiannon," he orders.

Reluctantly, I stand from my hiding spot. He flips on the light, and I squint against the fluorescent glare. He's scary when he's angry. Pinched face, flaring nostrils. And right now, he's madder than I've ever seen him. Hannah says to count when I'm afraid or upset and when I'm finished, it won't seem so bad. So, I count the steps over to him in my head to calm myself.

One.

Two.

Three.

I don't want to be a baby, but the tears start falling.

Four.

Five.

He grips my arm and yanks me in front of Xavier. "What are you doing here, Rhiannon?"

Through my tears, I answer. "I'm only eight, you can't expect me to make good choices."

He pulls his leather belt free from the loops… and then whips me.

Over and over.

Until the numbers in my head jumble.

Until I see little stars behind my squeezed eyelids.

Until I cry out I won't do it again.

"Stop," Xavier yells. "It's not her fault. Punish me."

"This *is* your punishment, Xavier," my father shouts.

Finally, after a few more minutes, the hits cease, but the sting and burn continues so fierce I rub my bottom. I'm sure Xavier really thinks I'm a baby now; I can't stop the shudders waffling my frame or the hiccuping sobs.

My father leans down, an inch from Xavier's stricken face, bracing his hands on the arms of the chair. "Remember this lesson."

Xavier doesn't look at me on the entire walk back. My father strides ahead of us across the lawn and when he's out of ear shot, Xavier takes my hand.

"One day, Rhiannon, I will take you away from him."

I don't say a word. The look in his eyes tells me he isn't kidding.

Grab your copy today **ON SALE: SHOP NOW**

Sneak Peek PLAYBOY

Here's where it all began. Read the first chapter of Jonah's story: PLAYBOY available now.

CHAPTER ONE

Jonah

"Did you get the prints over to marketing so the models can sign them for the meet and greet?" my overbearing boss Glenda asks.

"When have I ever failed you?"

She rolls her big, brown eyes, and I give her a slow wink.

Did I mention I'm a flirt? Kind of goes with the territory, I guess.

"Today there's a new model starting, so be nice." She smiles, showcasing a bit of an overbite.

"I'm always nice."

Glenda narrows her eyes at me, and I crack a smile.

"Yeah, that's what I'm afraid of," she mumbles under her breath, thumbing through a few pictures of a previous shoot in a folder in her hand.

I swing my legs off my desk, where I was comfortably

perched taking my mid-morning break, and check the lens on my Nikon. She's my baby, and I treat her well.

"Oh, and no long lunch today. The shoot is at two pm sharp." She pivots on her six-inch heels and glides from my office with the sophistication of a former model turned editor-in-chief. The last title is thanks to her husband, owner of *Bunny Hunnies*. Lucky break. In this town, sometimes it's not what you know but who you know.

But I don't need luck. I've got the dream job.

I stretch my arms over my head and stand. Chattering people pass my door on their way out to the shoot, so I grab my satchel, throw in my camera, and send a text to cancel lunch with my friends. Every Wednesday the four of us, Declan, Booker, Ethan, and myself, meet up. We've been best friends since high school, and ten years later, we're still the four horsemen. That was the name of our band in high school. And no, we don't play a single instrument.

It was more karaoke in Ethan's garage.

We thought we were the shit, though.

"Hi, Jonah," a few of the models walking into the Falcon building call out to me.

"Looking good, ladies." I wink and they giggle and smile.

I know you're thinking it. Have I slept with them? I'm not one to announce every girl I bang, I keep my sex life private, but, no, I don't mix business with pleasure. Zanna, Lyla, and Maria are off limits, no matter how much they try to tempt me.

I jump in my Jeep and head down to Venice Beach. Traffic is a bitch, but I finally ease into a parking spot and settle in to glimpse at the crashing waves. Living in LA is like living on a different planet. It's perfect weather all the time, ideal for photo shoots on the beach.

I spot the production crew down by the shore setting up, so I hop out of my Jeep and slip inside Hank's Franks, a local diner, and order a burger.

"Thanks, Gary," I say to the man behind the counter when

he hands me my bag of food. Ah, food. Real fucking food with grease and fat. This is what I need.

I step outside and chomp down on my burger while I watch the crew set everything out along the beach. My eyes zero in on the model. She's far away, but even from here her body's bangin.' She's not as tall as the other models and curvier.

Long blonde hair. Skimpy little pink bikini. Today's going to be a good day.

I finish off the burger, wash it down with a Coke, and head over before I lose the best light of the day.

"Jonah, over here," Tim, the shoot coordinator yells. "Meet Chelsea."

I drop my bag near the set and fish out my camera.

Her back is to me when I walk over, and I get a great view of her sweet ass barely covered by her bottoms.

She turns around and my jaw drops. Beautiful blue eyes I've seen countless times before stare back at me. Eyes I've known since I became best friends with her brother, Declan.

"Chelsea Sincock?" Fuck. Her last name suddenly takes on a whole new meaning. To say I'm shocked is an understatement. I was staring at her ass. At Declan's sister's ass. When did she grow up? I haven't seen her since their parents divorced and she moved to Texas with her mom at sixteen. Eight years ago. Declan mentioned she moved back a few months ago, but I had no idea she was modeling. How could he forget that detail?

"Oh my God, Jonah." She rushes over to fling her tanned arms around my neck. Her nearly naked body presses up against me, and I shake off how good it feels.

"What are you doing here?" I ask.

She releases her hold on me. "I'm the new model, obviously."

"Like hell you are." She can't model for this magazine. I hit the brim of Tim's ball cap as he ogles her. "Stop staring."

"Let me have your attention," I call out to the small crowd of set designers, makeup artists, and other crew workers. "No one's allowed to stare at her." But me. "This is my best friend's little sister."

Chelsea throws me a stunned glance. "Are you serious?"

"As a heart attack."

"Nice to know you've matured since last I saw you."

She's angry, hands on her curvy hips, and it's cute. Cute in a kid sister sort of way. Because that's all she is to me, a kid sister.

"Nice to know you have, too," I shoot back. The tone comes out all wrong. Sounds a little husky and sexual. Her body has definitely matured, and that's the problem. The pink triangles of her bikini barely cover her breasts. Does Declan even know?

He'd shit a brick if he knew. I need to tell him.

"Let's get started," I shout, yanking the cap off my camera and lining everything up for the shoot.

Chelsea gets into position, and I focus on her through the lens. The breeze lifts her blonde tresses, exposing the perfect symmetry of her face. High cheekbones, pert nose, full lips—my camera loves her. Now to figure out what to do with her. I want her in the water with the waves crashing over her body.

"Ok, make your way over to the shore. Dip your toes in."

She crosses the sand, and her tiny pink tipped toes dip into the waves rushing up the shoreline.

She shivers. "Oh, that's cold."

Her smile is perfect, and I snap a shot.

"She's gorgeous," Tim whispers next to me.

"Don't look at her," I warn over my shoulder. He thinks I'm joking but I'm not. I scan around at all the crew men's eyes gawking at her. "Guys, no staring," I remind them.

They laugh off my warning like it's some big fucking joke.

I really need to tell Declan. This is not ok. When she was younger, Declan and I would look after her when the kids would bother her. And now, a sense of over brotherly something or other is kicking in.

But, the more I aim my camera at Chelsea, the more I forget

she shouldn't be here. She's a natural at this. The sun kisses her skin, making my shot even better.

I loosen up, get into it—moving, shouting demands—and she follows every cue.

It's one of the best photo shoots I've had in a long time. Some of the other models have to be prompted to even smile. Most times, they won't react unless I say something to get them going.

But not Chelsea. No, she's really good.

Doesn't change my mind, though. I'm still telling Declan.

"Get all the way in the water," I direct, standing so close I'm almost right over top of her, snapping photo after photo. She does as told, and the shutter snaps furious and fast through every pose...

Stretched out on the wet sand, the frothy water rushing over her toned stomach.

Snap.

On her knees, beckoning with a seductive smile on her face.

Snap.

The waves crash at her back, and she loses her balance.

Snap.

She rises from the ocean.

Snap.

I drop my camera and rush forward, throwing my hands over her tits. "Cover your fucking eyes," I shout. "There's been a wardrobe malfunction."

Click here to grab your copy today.

About the Author

Logan Chance is a Top 20 Amazon and International Best Selling Author. A Goodreads Choice Award Finalist 2016, with a quick wit and penchant for the simple things in life: Star Wars, music, and pretty girls. His works can be classified as Dramedies (Drama+Comedies), featuring a ton of laughs and many swoon worthy, heartfelt moments.

For insights into his writing, games, awesome giveaways, and exclusive fun, sign up for his newsletter: Join Here
    Come join Logan on Facebook in his FB group: Join NOW

Don't be shy, follow Logan on all platforms:

Also by Logan Chance

The Playboy Series

PLAYBOY

HEARTBREAKER

STUCK

LOVE DOCTOR

A Mafia Romance

TAKEN

STOLEN, Coming Soon

THE ME SERIES

DATE ME

STUDY ME

SAVE ME

BREAK ME

Standalones

WE ALL FALL DOWN

GRAHAM

FLINGOLOGY, Part of the SPRING FLING ANTHOLOGY

THE BOSS DUET